A DESISTED CASE OF RAPE AND MURDER

A DESISTED CASE
OF RAPE AND MURDER

Clyde G Schultz

iUniverse, Inc.
Bloomington

A Desisted Case of Rape and Murder

iUniverse books may be ordered through booksellers or by contacting:

iUniverse
1663 Liberty Drive
Bloomington, IN 47403
www.iuniverse.com
1-800-Authors (1-800-288-4677)

ISBN: 978-1-4759-8095-0 (sc)
ISBN: 978-1-4759-8096-7 (e)

Library of Congress Control Number: 2013904301

Printed in the United States of America

iUniverse rev. date: 03/14/2013

THIS STORY WAS A DREAM, MARCH 24, 2010

The Victim; 12-year old Candy P Ploutz, Born April 10 1967. Place of the murder just off of County trunk, 36. Manchester Macon County, Georgia. The time April 15th 1979. The only suspect James L. Lundgrenn born May 4, 1962. A non-educated man dropped out of school in a third-grade. His mother, Mary J. Lundgrenn age 61 Born May 14, 1928 she had less educated than her son.

Police Lt. Investigator George Bingfang 42. District Attorney William W. Warsaw, age 39. Public defender Jeffrey P. Zachary age 41.

Prison cellmates Patrick R. Franklin, age 40, 280 pounds, and dark brown eyes

Billy E. Porter, 32. Alan Jeffers, 31. Ben Anderson, 41. David Dwyer, 28.

Case number 745 -- 362 -- 941 any resemblance to real people or places coincidental

CHAPTER 1

The Rape and Killing
of Candy P Ploutz

T his is just one of the cases that might show the abuse of power by a District Attorney's Office, and his staff that goes on all across America, at different times. When it was getting close to election time, and when they couldn't find any other suspects. The District Attorney ordered his staff and the Police Department; to desist their investigation of the murder of 12 year old Candy P Ploutz. Just three months after the murder, July 6, 1979, they charged the suspect James L. Lundgrenn 26 with rape and murder case number 745 -- 362 – 941.

The date of the murder, April 15, 1979, at 11 a.m. James L. Lundgrenn was riding his bicycle down a gravel road, and he spotted something lying on the road and then went to investigate; and found the murdered body of Candy L. Ploutz. James nailed down beside her naturally, he got blood on himself. He didn't know much about checking to see if a body was alive. So he ran back to his bicycle, and went to the nearest phone, which was a mile away he hurriedly called the 911 system, and of course he was excited, nervous, anxious, and upset, most anyone would be in that situation, and especially James. James was a poor boy dropped out of school in third-grade, and his mother also was very illiterate. At times he got jobs on a farm helping plant crops in the morning, or just shoveling cow manure.

Or any job he could get to help support him self, and his mother. I will be writing this story as if I were him. But it will not be his vocabulary that writes the story, and if you've never met any people that dumb; to put it bluntly, I have. When I was in the service back in 1946. The Young Man from Hope, Arkansas, he was actually that dumb, and he had a crust of dirt on his body. That was almost irremovable, some of the guys gave him the GIA shower, and the blood was pouring out of those tour membranes of skin. Just one more of those dumb slobs most people ignore. Let them go through their life, standby and watch it happened.

Don't care, is the word. Otherwise if we all care as much as we should, we wouldn't have these things happened. Maybe would not happen as often; and I think it's our responsibility, as human beings to stand up and say enough is enough. When you come face-to-face with these situations. Just the same night I dreamed the story was a program on Larry King live, that said it all about corruption of District Attorneys; and the 20-year incarceration of the wrong man, the DNA tests showed he was innocent. And his sperm didn't match the raped victim. I guess that's what prompted my dream, on the 24th of March 2010.

The 911 call; connected him with the sheriff department. James excitedly told his story of finding the brutally killed little Candy P. Plowtz. The sheriff said; you stay there and will pick you up in 15 minutes. When the sheriff arrived with his two deputies. The first thing they noticed was the blood on his blue jeans, and James had a stuttering problem. When he was excited, and naturally he was very excited that it even gave him an inferior complex, which he knew nothing about James told the sheriff, he lived with his mother and she was a very uneducated woman. When James was little, his mother receives child support pensions, but now they just lived on her widow's pension and whatever he could earn. So they lived very poorly had no modern television sets or things like that. The sheriff George Bingfang, handcuffed him, put him in the backseat of the squad car and told him to direct them to the spot where he found the body.

The body was just a couple hours old not much body heat loss. The sheriff ordered the crime scene marked off with yellow tape and called the Corner's office; and James was taken to police station immediately, and locked up. James had a lot of trouble answering all they're questions reasonably. And was not told of his legal rights? That he could have an Attorney present, when questioned. And of course, later, they deny that. And of course they thought he was guilty right from the start.

So they interrogated James, the rest of the day and into the night. And when he was so exhausted he could hardly keep awake; and couldn't think straight anymore. They drew up a shabby kind of confession, and James signed it just before they gave him something to eat. Of course, the police said it was voluntary, and meanwhile, a coroner was making examinations on the body. And so ended the first day.

April 16, 1979. The second day they took James over to the crime laboratory to make some examinations? And blood tests and had no discoveries, that James is blood matched the blood found at the crime scene was O positive. At the crime scene itself. They made no discoveries and blood trail leading into the woods and away from the body footprints close to a match to the footprints of James. Ever thing they found fit the description for James to be the suspect.

And they didn't believe one word, he told them. James told them he was coming back from the neighboring farm he went to asked for a job, and later his story didn't quite check out because nobody at the farm made any corroboration that his story was true. To verify that he even been there, and perhaps James had talked to a milk hauler. That day they took all the forensic evidence, and even pitchers of James his right leg was injured from the bicycle petal had a bruise as big as a quarter, and James said he got that morning from the petal of his bicycle going to that farm to look for a job.

The third day, the sheriff drove out to see James's mother, and when she saw the police. She fell to the ground. She was frantic; because her son did not come home for three days, she told the police that he never stayed anywhere overnight. She had no telephone to make any phone calls, and the sheriff finally told her what happened. He said, "We got your son locked up as a suspect for rape and murder." And of course, she wasn't formulary with the word rape, but she did know the word murder, and what that meant.

She had no money for lawyers, for any kind of defense funding for such a thing. The sheriff said, "We can hold him 90 days as a suspect. And he probably won't be getting out of their before that. We can have a public defender at your disposal, and he will come and see you soon." Mrs. Lundgrenn had no car to get around the store delivered their groceries, and supplies whenever they could.

The fourth day, July 10, more interrogation of James. Asking for more information asking why he would do something like this? And of course, James dozen know what to say, because he didn't know what the word rape meant or 75% of anything that they said to him. Just small details, so how could he answer the questions, he never know what the word sex meant so how can one answer questions correctly? If you don't know, the meaning of the words they were asking. James of course wasn't able to understand what happened to him? As a child that left him incapable of sexual things. But the labbitory never made any physical examination of his body, or establish any reasonable physical test that he was Impotent sexually. He had no way of telling the police, any things he did not understand.

The labbitory assistant took one look at James's penis; and knew it was impossible to get any sperm analysis, and all but made no record of that examination. The only blood was most normal O; Positive that matched the victim. So there was nothing written down about that examination. No record of any kind, let alone any sperm analysis or the fact that James was not circumcised; and due to the fact that James had the mumps, when he was just a young boy that ruptured both testicles. Thus it stunted, the growth of the penis itself, killing all sexual desire, and of course James knew nothing about this, all he knew he had to take it out of his pants to urinate.

Can any person be that ignorant? Some time, seeing is believing, and the criminalizes just botched up the job the only one assistant Jack Porter, 22 years old. Didn't admit he made some mistakes? And destroyed; the rest of the report. The only document, which could have helped James? And maybe cleared him of this terrible crime.

One week is gone by since the crime, and the public defender Jeffrey P. Zachary 42 years old. Finally goes out to meet James's mother. For the first time as he said, "Mrs. Lundgrenn. Your son is being held on suspicion of Rape? And murder case number 745 -- 362 – 941." Mrs. Lundgrenn didn't even know what to say to him. She was even had less education than her son James.

And she doesn't know anything that could help in her son's defense. The public defender, ask her all the questions you could think about their usual questions, but then nothing said that could help in any way. The public defender told her, all evidence that police have points to your son, and Mary Lundgrenn is devastated by his words, and the public defender says; he will do whatever he can to defend your son. But I'm going to need all the help I can get a need to know everything about James. From his childhood, anything you can tell me. If facts had been known at that moment this would have helped James's. But his mother did not know how to describe what happened to James when he was 12 years old. When the mumps had ruptured both testicles? And it would have made a big difference, if that had been known at that moment.

Important facts that could save a man's life if they were known at the trial? Meanwhile Mr. and Mrs. Daniel Poutz are screaming to the news media for justice for the District Attorney to make an arrest two months have went by, and the pressure that's involved for the District Attorney's office, must be tremendous enough pressure to turn good men into bad men.

CHAPTER 2

The Trial
The Order to Desist by the D.A.

The District Attorney is coming up for reelection in November. And not use to the pressure on him to do his job. So what's the life of this poor ignorant slob? He thinks? And who will care if he gets the wrong guy, and he somehow convinces himself that he has the right man. Another six weeks of pressure and still no other leads to any other culprits. He has to make the decision, he has got a shaggy confession, and the blood type, that is most common, and that the blood matches the blood on James's blue jeans of O positive. But there was no laboratory analysis to this case. But the DA did not know that some testing was disregarded by the Assistant of the laboratory. The only marks on James were a bruise on his right leg that he said he got ridding his bicycle.

Which the District Attorney never did believe, they said the bruise on his leg was caused by the victim, kicking him. The DA pondered his thoughts if this was enough to convict James for murder. When James was questioned by the investigators? he didn't actually know the meaning of the words involved in this case at all.

Two more weeks go by, now the third month, the pressure is enormous, and the DA called the sheriff to his office and ordered him to desist. All investigation of this case, 745 -- 362 -- 941, and he also ordered his staff to desist all investigation. The County Sheriff George Bingfang put up some effort to keep the case open. But he went directly to the jail; and arrested

James L. Lundgrenn for the rape and murder; of 12-year-old Candy, P. Ploutz July 6, 1979. The front page of the news paper said District Attorney Arrests, James L. Lundgrenn for the rape and brutal murder of 12-year-old Candy, P. Ploutz Macon County, Manchester, Georgia.

The body was found, April 15, 1979 at 11:45 a.m. So public defender was notified of the arrest, and was summoned to the jail, to speak with James. And he brought along a copy of the today's paper that showed all the incriminating evidence against him in the public opinion; was very strong that they had the right man. And the Assistant District Attorney makes his public announcement, to the press that they have a long strong case against James L. Lundgrenn; for the rape and brutal murder of Candy P. Ploutz. No trial date set yet, but could be within 30 days to public defenders told James he would go see his mother immediately, because she had no way of communicating with the public defender, and he would see her once a week and keep her posted on what was going on.

She did not know herself that she had information that could have helped her son James. She was tormented constantly by the public and harassed daily by the townspeople at night, as well as in the daytime. She asked the public defender, Jeffrey P. Zachary, for some protection or if there was something he could do to stop this. But no protection was available, all you could say was, this will lighten up as time goes on and he told her to be patient. But she didn't know the meaning of the word.

It's a constant intrusion for people like Mrs. Lundgrenn. One can hardly imagine what she's going through; she trusts that her son was not capable of such a crime against anyone. But words can hardly describe Mrs. Lundgrenn, and her son, James both so ignorant of life and so many things, things that could have stopped this terrible ordeal; this terrible rush to judgment, by the District Attorney's Office. And she claims they have the wrong man for the DA had built his case, and relentlessly pursued the case against James L. Lundgrenn. And D. A. gave daily television interviews to the public. The public defender did not ask for a change of venue, for his client. and the date was finally picked for August 22, 1979. There were no witnesses involved to testify to anything.

The only cross examination was all of the police report itself. That was made very incriminating with a signed confession by James? And they showed the only pitcher of James's right leg. Apparently bruised by the victim, kicking him, and they didn't bring up the bicycle that he rode that day it vanished. Whenever James said, "That he had road, his bicycle to that farmer to ask for a job." Now that was ever mentioned. And there was nothing that Jeffrey P. Zachary could do at this time. Two day's trial almost two at least, said today showed the blood work from the victim.

And they showed the O positive blood taken from James L. Lundgrenn. Seemed almost enough to convict, and find him guilty. and James just sat there with a numbed mind. And his mother just sat there behind him, crying the entire time. The news people reported each day's events and the third morning. James was found guilty by the jury and sentenced to death. But since Georgia had revoked the death penalty, six years ago for Judge sends him to life without parole. That meant at least 50 years for James, if you live that long, since the body was found by a road, the state was involved, as well as the FBI, and since no missing child report was filed, the FBI waiver of their jurisdiction; and a case against James L. Lundgrenn, sent him to state prison at Columbus, Georgia.

James actually was just another poor victim himself; that happen to stumble onto a body lying alongside the ditch of a county road, but couldn't prove his innocence. And in this country you are supposed to be innocent until proven guilty, not the other way round, just think what this poor ignorant wretch of a man will have to endure in the prison system for 50 years. Not a strong built man, more like a meek person.

CHAPTER 3

James is Sentenced
to Life in Prison

August 30 James was taken by bus to the penitentiary for life. He arrived at the prison, at 11 a.m. and after his induction a cold bath, after examination of his upper body only was given a number 180 given the usual prison necessities of clothes and bathing utensils and was assigned to bed number six in Cell 172 cellblock D. Mostly they all life imprisonment members in this block long hardened criminals, and very much use to prison life.

James had a little good luck in that cell which 5 other men. And they like him immediately and would look out for him. The biggest man in the cell said, "Young fellow, we are all you got," his name was Patrick R. Franklin, age 40, 280 pounds, dark hair brown eyes and a strong easy-going, not hot tempered big man. The oldest man was Bernard D. Anderson, 41 years old, 180 pounds light hair blue eyes.

William C. Porter, age 32, 165 pounds, dark hair blue eyes, David T. Dwyer, age 28, 170 pounds, light brown hair, Allen J. Jeffers, age 31, 160 pounds. Light hair blue eyes, he was studying to become a lawyer, and in a few days they all seem to get along real well together as a group and would keep it that way at all costs.

Prison life is a daily routine, dressed by 6:30 a.m. breakfast at seven, work time tell11:40 a.m. luncheon at 12 p.m. sharp, and afternoons, recreational outdoor activity till 3:30 p.m. and then back to your cell or studies, if you have a permit for the library or things like that the lights out by 8:45 p.m. religious services on Sunday, and all members will attend no special denomination, medical checkups once every 90 days unless of complaints, and that they did the second day, but again, it was not a complete examination; of James's entire body, the usual shots for medical reasons and then back to your cell with your own time.

James now has to learn how to conform to their sense of conformity. They actually rob the prisoner of the most important thing in his life. His own individuality, but here everyone is innocent. But that's a good thing because it helps keep them to endure their unending torment is a matter of adjustments, some men are quick to make that adjustment and others are not, the people that run the prison system, they believed their right, and most of the prisoners, are forced to comply with their conformity to life. And it's not easy for any individual to make that adjustment.

Only time you will see any medical person now is if you have any medical complaints for any examination, and sometime get shots for medical purposes. Sometime you have time just for reading only, that is if you're capable of reading, which James was not in any manner shape or form, but he never read a book. Allan and James in just a short time became very good buddies.

When James told Allen, that he only had a third grade of schooling. He became interested in trying to help James, in whatever way he could, and James stuck with the men like they were his brothers or next of kin, and soon became best friends. And he soon saw what could happen to him out in the yard. And if you didn't stay together as a group. And he made unshakable bonds in just a short time. State penitentiary's are the roughest prison systems of all, I know I read somewhere myself sometimes, or when I heard it. That 60% that get paroled from the state penitentiary comeback. They can't make it on the outside, they do not get rehabilitated in any manner shape or form; some of the man been there near 15 years. Even get worse than they were when they came in the first time.

Prison life is long and hard. Some of them were there a long time, Bernard Anderson. He was here 16 years. He was just 16 when he was sent to Georgia State penitentiary. 16 years ago, and Like I said, everybody is innocent in these places, and the smart thing to do is to stick with the group, Alan Jeffers, a high school graduate, was the smartest one of the group. He was sent here five years ago, and they said he killed his girlfriend in a jealous rage. Five years ago at age 24, but he said he knew who it was that killed his girlfriend. And he was trying to get himself an education. My reading the law books, and hopes he could prove his own innocence someday.

Rehabilitate comes from the Latin word meaning to restore within one's own reputation. Which one has launched to put back in good condition. But most prison systems do not, I am no expert on prisons and thus what I'm saying may not be true. But I don't have to be 100% accurate.

Allen took an instant liking to James and wanted to help get him a better education. When James told Allen he only went to the third-grade, but he said it'll take time. Life is slow in a prison system to get the time to study with all the checks. We have during a 24-hour day. It's almost impossible, getting the time to study. First thing we got to do is get you a library card. So you can check books in and out, we'll start with third-grade literature and move up from their but believe me, James we'll do it. You and I together, friends James said, "OK friend. And I'm willing to learn everything I can". The warning lights at lights out, and study time was over and lights out.

Just imagine in school. It takes eight hours a day, 9 1/2 months a year to pass just one grade. In prison it will take 10 times that long to finally get his high school diploma, or they'll said will work every hour, we can find to that level of education at all to wonder to continue his education, and it is a law degree as well. So they made a good pair a good team. One day is a long time in the prison system. I've never been in a prison system, or even visited one thank God. But I did serve a short time in county jail once a long time ago a young lad a few years ago and was arrested for a drunk walking charge, which I thought at the time they was overstepping their authority. Find me $35 or 10 days in jail, and I wanted to make a point to the judge that I thought they were wrong. And I refuse to pay the fine. And I served the 10 days in jail. So I know a little bit about that kind of routine, and most county jails treat you fairly well, because you're not a hardened criminal, but in State penitentiary in a week must be endless for young man like James, replied Patrick.

Allen of course he's been there five years in prison, time is hard, but you get used to it, to the daily routines and nights its lights dim. Before 9 p.m. up early and breakfast by 7 a.m. cellblock D is close to the kitchen and dining area, but they follow a pattern with cellblock changing from time to time. And then there's some that get their meals served in the cellblock itself. And of course he was on our punishment in the hole 30 days in the hole is a lifetime, and there isn't many that go without the punishment and that is exactly the point, it's easy to get into that kind of trouble. If someone else starts the fight with you. So you both get 30 days in the hole. You have to conform to their ways and their example of right and wrong. Not your own individuality, conforming to those set of rules is the hardest thing for any prisoner.

James only had his mother on the outside, and he was allowed to write her 2 times a month, and his public defender, lawyer never even called him and his mother could not afford to come and see him or help them in any way. So with no one on the outside, it's hard for a convict to get help. Or even a sense of support from someone on the outside with a sense of loss and hopelessness that soon. It is hard to keep your spirits alive, that awful hopeless, insecure trap. The trap that binds you if you are caught like a rat in the trap. That was James statement, and only he was capable of saying, and thus it made your mind to hate. What society has done to you because you know, you are innocent. You can't help but feel hatred for society, for putting you in such a terrible place. And it's no wonder that 60% parolees come right back.

But Allen told him, where there's life there's hope, as she should do every weekend to fight those feelings and try hard to keep some open mind that some day we both will walk out of here free men. And cellblock D was all kinds of hardened criminals, not just murderers, some would come and go, but most of them were for longtime.

Now 30 days have passed is now September 30. A cold morning for the climate of Georgia. They have usually warmer weather still in September. And this afternoon at a soft ballgame outside after lunchtime is an organized game by the prisoners themselves. So many players that sometimes you don't even get up to bat. But they all participate and get some fun out of the exercise, and it is also good for their bodies. And they usually all have to attend unless they are sick and can't attend these events. And once in awhile, they get to see the warden. And the medical officer check ups each prisoner once every 90 days or so, unless they complain.

They get clean clothes once a week, two baths's a week, two time's week to the library if you have a library card. Time is limited, but you can check out books and take them to your cell, and they will be returned by carrier once they're locked up in your cell. You are responsible for those books, and you are not from your pay if damage comes to those books and there are other harsher penalties and your card could be taken away.

The next month, James wrote his mother for the very first time, a short letter in third-grade language. But then his mother couldn't read anyway, but I'm sure she'll find someone to read it for her, and James was happy and proud that he could even write a letter.

I remember my first letter to my mother and father, when I was inducted into the service to 1946 and went to Japan. Just nine months after they dropped the atomic bomb on Hiroshima, and it was carried there by a big bomber, the Enola Gay, August 6, 1945. And I remember all the lonely feelings I had while in the middle of the ocean. Surrounded With 1700 men.

And some of the saying is James told his mother after 61 days of incarceration, seemed a lifetime already, one day in the prison yard, some big guy got mad at James and started pushing him around and big Patrick; came to his rescue shoved this big fellow only ending the ruckus for the time being. And you don't want to be out there alone in that situation. But James was starting to like this big man like a brother. With all these good feelings, he felt that he had someone who cared, and someone who understood perhaps even better than he did himself. But feelings good about men and not in any way being gay sense of mind and James heard the word for the very first time, but didn't know what it meant. And that evening, he asked Al, what it meant.

Don't think it's impossible, because as a farm boy. When I went to the service. I did not know that there were even people like that. Nor did I know the word, homosexual or gay, or queer, and that doesn't mean you're abnormal if you don't know what James was truly abnormal stunted by a childhood disease. Crippled from the malformation of a disease called mumps, and what they can do to a child's sexual hormone. Of course James knew none of this.

And if he would've been questioned in a proper manner. Probably never would have wound up in this prison system, told Allen didn't know anything about that kind of stuff. He called it Allen said, "You never made it with a girl" James said, "Made what", Allen said, "I'll explain to you like this in words, you can understand." You ask why they do if something like this, Allen said, "It's hard to explain, but men make love two women or girls by using their penis."

James said, "What is a penis," Allen said, "Take that thing out of your pants, would you urinate with. So James took out his thing and showed it to Al. His penis. He also said, "I, just pea out of this thing. When he pulled it out of his pants, and it wasn't much more than 2 inches long." Allen said, "My God man, you weren't even circumcised at all so how to hell did you rape and kill that 12 year-old girl."

James said, "They said that same word, but what is it. I don't even know the meaning of these words they used. And I still don't know anything of these things that you just told me." Allen said, "Now I do believe you. James and I promise you that I will help you prove that it was physically impossible for you to commit this crime. And get you out of this place if it's the last thing I do. You cannot even get an erection so it's impossible for you to have committed such a crime that they said that you did.

Allen said, "What we talked about this afternoon, I don't want you to mention one word, to no one. Hell man did they ever examine you before your court hearing before your trial." And James said, "I don't remember much. Nothing like you just showed me. I still don't understand of what it's all about," Allen said, "Take your time. It's going to come to you, but be patient, and it will take us a few years to get you educated enough and myself. So we would just bide our time and don't tell a single soul about what's going on for you and I."

So James said, "OK."Allen said, "Anybody finds out, that could jeopardize our cases. If anyone finds out even in our cell, they might not understand, so mum is the word. And it's just you and I OK, partner James felt a little string of hope. By his own words, and he was trying very hard to understand it all. Allen felt so sorry for James had earlier said, "That he felt sorry for that little girl." And now trying to understand it all what they said he had done. He didn't quite understand just what it was all about, but he knew what murderer was or killing something."

He seen some of that on the farm that he worked on. I didn't do any of that myself. But I seen it done on the farm, and it was starting to remember other things from farm and what they called breeding of the cattle; and I know what a bull was. And I was just started to understand, as you started to come to be breeding of the cows. And I started to realize what Allen said when he showed me his big penis. I never saw anything like that and he used the word circumcised, whatever that meant, he said that they cut off a little tip of your penis and somehow that is called able to strip the skin back over the head of your penis and is called having sex. And somehow I still don't get it.

But Allen said, "Just take your time, and I promise you will remember everything there is to know and the answer is to teach you all these things. So you know about sex, and everything else. And someday all the pieces of the puzzle are going to fit together in your mind when you are ready to accept all these things. And we get ready to make our move to free you from a crime you did not commit. If we can overturn your conviction, and that will take a lot of work and a lot of years to come about. And you and I are going to do it when I passed my law degree. You will be my first client. You got any money. James said, "I got $.50, "Allen said, "Give it to me. This is my first half of a dollar, and it will bind a contract. You are now officially my first client, and I sure I will get you out of this place someday or die trying."

Allen Strong words gave me some hope to cling to. To survive my ordeal, day by day, month by month, year after year. I was doing good Allen said in school, and he was going to move me up to the fourth-grade going to only one step at a time and not overanxious. He said, be patient, and I was just starting to learn what that word meant. And he was using a lot of words I didn't understand, and of course in third grade, you don't get words like that, or fourth-grade, or why they even say them.

James was like a big grown up kid in the fourth-grade with that level of schooling, Allen said, "It takes time to get this all squared away in your mind". But I already know a good specialist that can prove beyond any doubt that your genitals were ruptured at an early age of 12 years old and could not function in the normal manner. Or get an erection so why would you have bothered this little girl. If there's no motive. You could not have committed the crime. And if you can prove you were at that farm that's an alibi; at that same moment. It will take some investigating? Before I'm able to submit your case to defend you from the crime, they said you committed.

CHAPTER 4

Allen Studding to be an Attorney

Allen was saying it will be hard to prove my own case, that they claim I murder my girlfriend. But there was someone else involved, someone else was there that night? After he left her; he admitted that they had an argument. He'll have to find him. I have someone on the outside that is able to help me. And none of Allen's blood was found on the crime scene. And Allen has B positive blood, hers was O positive. And they had no sexual relations for 40 hours prior to that night.

Allen thought she was cheating on him. And after there argument, left, and whoever was there came out of the closet. And his girlfriend wanted to break their relationship off with him and he got mad and beat her up and killed her. His friend on the outside will do all his investigating for him. But it's going to take a lot of time; I guess maybe even five years, or six. But when we are ready, I promise you, we can win this fight.

Allen ask me about the District Attorney, if he up for election in November? Yes, I answered, Allen said, "There is a real strong chance that he filed the charges against you, with his election in mind. It would synch the election for him and he gambled that no one would care whether some poor slob like you would be sent to jail and it could be just a case of rush to judgment. And chinch his reelection." I said, "His name was William W. Warsaw," Allen said, "Let's start a file on Mr. Warsaw. We hide it along with their other stuff behind our toilet did a perfect spot to ride our record book but we can't afford to lose them."

And James I want you to remember everything, your plans to begin story from day one. And ill write down everything from the police investigation? Through the District Attorney Department, and the laboratory investigation? These were Allen's words not mine.

Allen wrote down everything in a small notebook, and he wrote in small letters, very readable, and I put down everything I could remember Al wrote mine out for me said I was improving with my studies, and I would learn third-grade and we studied every available hour we could find, and until the others too much or what we're thinking or studying and didn't tell the other four guys in our cell. He added these notes are important and this is the name of our game, secrecy is the word, Al also were studying law books and made a joke to the others that he was practicing law ought to get himself out of this place.

Now seven months have past since now March 30th 1980. Meanwhile they had their usual shakedowns? And we try to keep our sell clean and free from any unauthorized material. From time to time they find things, like made knifes. But our hiding place was just behind the toilet bowl. Admittedly, he started his notebook and used a painted cardboard to hide it in place within them the lot of time to just be alone and that would be the time that we would write our notes. They're studying time came first, Patrick called us both book worms, but that was ok with us, so don't let that bother you James okay.

One day Allen brought a new book from the library, the name said. The Imbalanced Hormone. And he said this is the very book. That's going to get you out of this place. He read me a paragraph that said, one of man's testicles are crushed or ruptured. It is physically impossible for him to get an erection. Because that also killed, the glam that produces testosterone, a substance ever man has to have if he is going to get an erection. Today there's help for people like this, with testosteral shots Addrodirm or even Viagra. All leaves more room substances is part of the problem that you have James and not being circumcised. You have never stretched your skin back? on your penis did you.

I said, "I knew nothing. All I knew I had to urinate out of it." What year did you have those mumps. Do you remember I said, "I think, in between 12 and 13 Mom put some hot flax seed between my legs. It hurt like hell, must have been a week, at least."

My mom showed me how to wash it out with my finger, every time I took a bath, Allen said, "Now here is the case we have to build for you that it was physically impossible; for you to get an erection, and therefore there was no motive for the raping and killing of that little 12 year-old girl. It sounds very simple. When I say it and if the doctor for the District Attorney's Office would have made this examination, he could have determined that and you wouldn't be here today and that's the case. The exact case. We have to make this one thing to match blood up stuff like that. But were there two doctors by any chance involved in the investigation against you.

Their could have been, but it was not at a hospital or a clinic. I think they called it a laboratory is all I can remember, Allen said, "Well. There wasn't much for them to get rid of then," I said, they take one pitcher of my right leg and show that in court. So the DA didn't have much of anything to rush to judgment about, will prove to be very annoying for Mr. Warsaw. And hopefully we can get him disbarred." That's the best we can hope for Allen said, "You said you signed some kind of paper like the confession." That's what they called it I said, and that's what they told me. When I never ever said that I did it. I just got real confused and upset and frustrated. You told me those word yourself if in fact, and were his own words," Allen said, "Yes. Those were the right words, and I will come up with more words. And I sent a message to my friend outside in code."

I also sent him to your town to talk to that farmer; you said you ask for a job that day. I set up this code with him awhile back. So we can communicate and I have been sending him names by one letter at a time he knows what to look for. And I can write only to times a month to the same person. He can't tell me much in his return mail, because we don't know what the prison guards will read and sanction out of my letters. So we got to be damn careful. The lights went dim meaning 20 minutes lights would be out and bedtime. Allen put the box away for tonight, James tomorrow is another day.

The guard made his rounds, and all of us in cell 172, were in bed. Allen on the meddle bunk and I was in the top bunk, and the bunks are 3 High so we could talk softly to each other. Without disturbing the others. Morning brings a new day with the usual routine. And for some of us just another hard days work. But you get used to that as well from the dining area and go directly to work, and after lunch a few hours outside. And in late afternoon library and study hours until suppertime, and another day is almost over. And a few hours are valuable study time to lights out, and another day is gone in the life of a convict.

Everything that Allen wanted to accomplish, and one day at a time it we'll take many days. And we wouldn't dare rush this process. He warned me over and over and to keep the fate and be patient. And I was learning those two words very well, since I've been here, I was learning in a very fast fashion. And that's what Allen thought at first and a move me up to fifth grade studies. And we didn't spend too much time on mathematics. He said, that will come later, slowly drew you once, you can count to what ever and subtract and multiply a bit Allen said, "I got her to teach this boy everything as he was talking to Pat, and meant it as a joke.

Al got a letter from his outside contact, saying that he had two possible suspects. That could have been in his house on the night his girlfriend was murdered. He said, "One of the girlfriends that worked with Lavon said she found a couple of phone numbers, in her old desk drawer pasted upside down on the top of the drawer and it was telephone numbers and both from the same town that one of Buna Vista Georgia. When I call that one guy, he flipped his cork when I mentioned the name Lavon, and I'm going to search his building this week to see what I could come up with will let you know, next month. Old friend and signed it just a friend Roy.

So Allen had read me the letter twice, and you look happy for the first time in a long time. That's my first good news I had since I've been here, and it had made him smile and he said, well my friend James our file is getting bigger. And I got to keep these letters that is while I hide the notebook, but they do let you keep letters. If you want to and want to start a scrapbook and I'll figure that out later. And I ask him what he called was Allen said it's like a roadmap that tells you where to go. The lights went dim, and another day was coming to an end. Patrick said, "What are you two mumbling about," and Allen said, "Do you trust me. I am studying to be an Attorney and believe me; OK and Patrick said okay Pal." Allen said, "You can be my second client, for one carton of cigarettes, and OK." And Patrick said, "You got a deal, and my mouthpiece hasn't done anything for me in a couple of years."

And some day you can tell me more of the details of your case. You can do me another good flavor by keeping this quiet and help us guard my boy James. Like you did out in the yard. I don't want him hurt anymore than he already has. He has endured enough problems now for a young man. Okay.

Patrick said, "I'll keep an eye on him for you, and also, you know that big fellow in the yard. Six months ago, said he wanted to make James his lover", Allen said yes, I heard that myself. And that's why I want you to be close to him when were out in the yard. James just does not understand these things as we do, while lights went out ending another day in 10 months since James came into this prison system, and Patrick James really didn't do anything. I want you to know that he is innocent of all these trumped up Chargers that were brought against this poor boy. He didn't even understand the word of rape and murder let alone do such a terrible crime, and I have good evidence to prove it to add all this to his case.

And I trust you Patrick that you will help me in every way you can, and Patrick promised that he would do so, tomorrow is inspection day again, and the wardens want us to paint our cell, next week, you and I have been chosen, because we had some painting experience on the outside. Allen said, "James and I will help and James needs some on-the-job training and something for the future" To get a decent job when he gets out of this rotten joint. And that's a start in the right direction, and that was the last word, as the lights went out. We all slept pretty well because of the long day and hard work. When you're tired you fall asleep fast, and we all get plenty of that in here. And before you know what it was morning.

Morning was just another day of push and shove to get dressed, in the one half hour we have each day, in a normal day of the year, all in a mad rush to shave and get dressed in half an hour six men to wash up in one basin and one toilet. But Allen worked out a plan that works very well for us all the time and a good savor of time. I let the tallest man and the shortest man shave at the same time, Pat and Alan shave at the same time, and I am shorter than Ben, and then the last two. And we manage fairly well to make that all in 30 minutes. And we keep our cell, very clean. And we always passed inspection, every time and had a good record so far. And we all worked very hard to keep that and they all respect Allen's leadership.

And they're just starting to respect me also. And they all consider me their boy. I'm not really that much younger.

Breakfast this morning we had French toast and eggs, coffee and jelly and jam, and only two hours worked time for some reason, but no outside activity because it was raining so that meant ill have a longer day to do our inside study time. And just a short inside calisthenics, and James and I could get at his valuable study. Education time, and Allen would have also some time to work on the law books, he got a plan for next week when we have to paint this cell room, he got the idea last night to build a safe, and remove the cement block underneath the toilet by taking that block out completely. It will slide out easy cut it in half and then we all have to distribute the excess cement on the outside, and I think this can be done easily, and I found some new putty that does not get hard. It's like gum and it will give me 6 by 12 inches of space to hide my papers. And you can reshape it each time between the blocks, and we have six by twelve inches of space to hide the papers so they're are safe, that they won't know anything about it next week I will design it while we have materials to do. The painting. So after calisthenics we got directly at the books. Allen brought fifth grade material now.

Allen said, "I think I can take one year off my prediction, and with a little luck, maybe we can overturn that trial of yours in less time we got a good prison record now and that will help us." Most when the time comes, we find ways to have our own birthday parties and such things like that or each month, all six of us save something from our lunch of cake or pie at lunchtime. Everybody brings something on that day, and later that evening after supper we have our birthday party.

So we got a lot done today on that day that Allen always cautioned us to take one day at a time, and mark it on our calendar, good or bad. We passed inspection early that morning, and the guard gives us a one-year plaque to hang on our wall. And a perfect record. And later that day, from the medical pharmacy, Allen managed to steal a bottle of grain alcohol and mixed with a soda pop and water. We had almost 2 quarts to drink and James got drunk for the first-time.

Allen said at one urge you to become a man and know your limit and your own personal choices. We all have to do it each and every day, and it was the best time I ever had. And James had some tears coming down as he said, "It was just the boos that I drank" I said I had a bottle of wine one time on the farm outside of our town so I do know what this stuff in it really is. My mother got someone to write me the letter, and Alan read it to me and I cried again, Allen said, "You'll get more used to these good things, as well as the bad things. You just have to learn to handle both. I said, "The wardens said I was adjusting real well. And so did the doctor."

We all wrote our birth dates on a calendar each time they brought us a new one. The lights dimmed, and it was time for lights out again in 20 minutes so we better cleanup our cell before bed. Patrick was already in bed, said he had a sore back, and Ben was working on him with hot towels. We all take a part in helping each other out, from time to time with muscle aches and pains that we cannot take care of ourselves.

And we all try very hard to keep personnel, very clean and healthy, because we realize it's important for everybody to keep the others in our cellblock clean. Patrick said I should study harder to become a doctor and laughed a bit. But that's part of it to keep each other healthy, even Billy Porter was more interested in cleaning.

And on Monday morning, they brought us a cart full of paint, and canvas paint rollers, everything you could think of that we needed to paint the cell. I got at the chipping of the blocks, and it didn't take long I had that block completely out. In another hour I had it cut in half but was another problem to get rid of all the waste material and directed them to take care of that problem. When he pinned his pants legs together and filled up both most of it out that way he carried out in one trip. While I had the block back in the hole and my papers, safely tucked inside. And when they returned, we had that part of the wall painted in reasonable time. And by noon, we were almost done by the time Jim Westphal the prison guard gave us a well done. We got new bedding and clothing for everybody in the prison system, they always use an oil-based paint, which has a high odder, and not easy to get rid of, their not adopted to latex paint that dries real fast. And in the afternoon we had still four hours of study time, while four of the guys played cards. Allen James of course had no time to play cards. We were busy every hour we could possibly find at studying our lessons. And we let them know we didn't have time for cards.

I was able to write my mother a nicer letter this time, and Allen used it as a class project and checked my grammar and spelling. He gave me a big list of words. I was supposed to memorize bigger words than you find in fifth grade class and to memorize my case number 745 -- 362 -- 941, and I really did remember that number, and Allen also remembering the word rape. And what that meant, and the word sex, and what men and women do to each other for fun, they called it, Allen said, "They may do this for other purposes like having babies like you said about your cows on the farm. But you could learn all these words, in time."

Allen said, "If I can educate you to 8th grade level. I could then make my move. If we can organize a series of doctor examinations, and that would start the overturning of your case," one-day Allen came back from the library and had a big book with him and he said this is the very book. That's going to change your case, and I told him that I had a sore on end of my penis, and he took a look at it, and offered some kind of the petroleum jelly and that he put that on. The book said hormone malfunctioned an early age and the devastation of childhood diseases.

Allen also said, "This is the very book that can help me prove your case, and I marked all pages that can help us. But I need one more book called after effects of childhood diseases of mumps and its treatments, and we need examinations of your penis and testicles documented examinations for our case, and I think I've found just the man to help us." He's a young man named Jesse Wright. He's an intern at the infirmary, and next week I'll talked to him about your problem, and he wants to make an incision near your testicles to find out what happened to them testicles. And I ask if he could make a record for us of his findings. And he agreed to do so, on the QT so we got lots to think about next week.

New day Sept. 15 1981 just another ordinary day in the prison system, at least, it started out to be just an ordinary day. As we stepped out of our cell to march to the mess hall, and we had a good breakfast of pancake sausage, eggs and coffee, and a lecture from the second-in-command of the prison system on good behavior. And some of us were given our appreciation for that good behavior. And our cellblock was given a higher rating, and of course this is designed to get some of the others to do better in their cell blocks. But nevertheless they have to keep order, and there's many different ways of doing just that.

And then there are some of the inmates they resent the fact that you were rewarded and your good behavior. And of course, some take their own actions for your doing better and supposed to make them do better for any reason they can conjure up. We were allowed extra time this morning for our shower, as it was bath day for our unit. So it was part of our true reward for good behavior. But then privileges are not easy to come by, but easy to lose. Just make the wrong move on the outside and in the hole you go for 30 days. And there went your hard earned privileges.

Their were only a few colored men in our cellblock, but they keep them segregated, and I didn't know any of those words either or why some people didn't like colored people. And I never was able to figure it out. Of course Allen didn't know either, he usually knew everything. I know that I trust him and think the world of him. He is my knight in shining armor, and I learned the meaning of many words, while I was listening to him. He was now studying under fifth grade material, but there's no room for child play in this situation, but true events can be so hard for him to explain to me when I am making lots of progress. And I can ask him at any time, questions which he tries to answer patiently, and especially questions about black men. And why they are segregated. I used that word again, and I did not understand.

I don't understand it even now, after he explained it the second time. He simple said it will come to me someday. Allen said, "Not to visit them" But in the yard that afternoon, I was visiting with half a dozen black men, and I liked all of them. And when I was going back to our own area, one of the big men in cell 180 called me a Nigger lover. Of course I didn't know what that meant, but the man cracked me and busted my nose, and they had too rush me to the medical center, where they had to set and bandage my nose.

CHAPTER 5

Allen is Convinced
James is Innocent

Allen didn't know where I was and he was getting nervous and he likes to keep an eye on me as much as he could, and it took him time to run me down, they had my nose set and bandaged and fully taped all way around. I told the doctor what happened and they at least sent a guard to put that man in the hole. I was finally allowed to go back to my cell with Allen and he said. "From now on, I want you to stay with Pat or Bernard." When you're outside so I promised Allen, I would do that.

Because he was worried; when he couldn't find me for a couple of hours. And of course, Allen wanted to know the details of what happened. And of course, I explained all that I didn't understand in the first place. And why this man got so mad that I visited with these colored men for a time. I said I don't understand why some men get so mad that those nice people I liked all of them and they like me. Allen said, "Maybe next time it won't happen this way, but maybe you better not do that very often."

Cellblock B and cellblock D. and E. the guards open them with keys passed down from above on a long cord. And once in awhile, some prisoner tries to crawl up to one of the other cells, and of course when they missed the cell count. The prison system naturally went into a prisoner missing system. We have sex cell counts in a 24-hour period. Of course the three meal times, and one in after noon, one at 11 p.m. and one at 3 a.m...

25

James didn't get any punishment for his part in that action, but that they put the bully 30 days in the hole for busting my nose, and a bath with the water hose. Allen said well that should cool him off and let's get at your schooling for the rest of the day.

What's left of it, I was very worried about you today and I got a visitor coming later this afternoon at 2:30 p.m. I think its Bob Bailey. That's my investigator on the outside, my friend and I can trust him. And he gave me a list of stuff I should study while he's gone, and stay in the cell, Pat will watch over you. He said he would keep an eye on you and the dinner bell sounded loud and clear, and the noise in the cellblock is unbelievable, at that time, with all the prisoners moving, and the clashing of the bars as a cell's open each block and the guards loud voices shouting orders, but today we had a good special meal steak and mashed potatoes beans gravy and green salad, bread coffee or tea milk or even both. If you wanted some time, we didn't have much choice is that we could make on our own.

At 1:30 p.m. Allen went directly to the visitor's entrance, and I was back in the cell and the rest of our mates went to the yard doing their physical activity. But Allen thought it was more important for me to study and being locked in, and nothing can hurt me inside the cell. Patrick would surely look out for me if I was outside.

Patrick never finish school, either he had about a six grade level of education. I think that's what he told me once and he was a house painter and said he would teach me how to become a house painter and give some job experience. He also said he had five more years here, may be less if he has good behavior, and he's working for that goal. I ask him what he did to get in here, and he said he wrote out a lot of checks that bounced. And finally got it for embezzlement.

That's a federal crime also checks went out by mail sometime it's not the matter of how much I do one to five and then got in trouble here and they tacked on four more. So He made a joke about my nose, as he looked at my big bandaged nose. But don't do anything to get in more trouble. Okay and I said, "Patrick old Buddy I got studying to do" Allen gave me a list of stuff to study. What town do you live in, Patrick said, "Weston, Georgia south and 150 miles or so?

I got married once, didn't last long" I said, "My father run off when I was just a little boy got himself killed, jumping off of a freight train.

No insurance mother got just a little pension from the only place he ever worked, and the government. When I was 10 or so, so I quit school. And got a job to help mother, with the expenses on the house.

At 3:30 p.m. Allen came back from visitors, section he was very excited about something and said, "Bob had some very important things, about this guy that was at my house that night that my wife Sandy was killed. And Bob went to his house made an investigation. It really was an old shack more or less and found some letters from Sandy and he took pictures of those letters, and he found a dress of Sandy's. Maybe the one she wore that evening, unless she had two of the same," and also Bob said, he went to that farm and the owner said he knew you and would ask everyone on his farm. If they remembered you being there at that time on that day.

He said, "You may have talked to one of the milk hauler's. And he would also find out about that." And he also had some good things to say about you, and even believe you didn't do such a terrible crime. And you were a good worker. And nothing but good things to say about you, so he is definitely on your side and Bob also did a study on. The District Attorney and he definitely was up for election that next November. And won the election by a landslide. And he also wrote down the name of the intern. That worked in that laboratory, that technician Joseph Pollack, 23 years old, first-year on-the-job and he remembered nothing of the incident of your examination, but when you get someone like him under oath, he may tell the truth, writing a book and looking for information about your case.

And of course, the sergeant was not helpful at all and the only things they said were incriminating things. Nothing that will help your case, until we get them on the stand, and how is your nose feeling. I said, "When the medication war off. It hurts a lot." Allen said, "I'll have the guard get you some from the dispensary may be at suppertime. And that's only on hour from now, and it will be another 30 days before I can see Bob began.

He's going to send someone to see me, but it takes 30 days to get on your visitor list and prove they have a right to visit you. He said he was a cousin of mine, and the man is Bob Bailey and he'll have information to pass along to me. And when you see him, you can pin that information under your lapel of your shirt, and it will be of course, in my code.

So suppertime bell rang and the crash of bars opening seamed louder than before for some reason, and Allen asked the guard for some pain pills for James. And they gave him enough to last him through the night and a good dose for the moment, which takes a while to take effect. With a good supper and back to the cell 172, and a few hours it will be lights out, but just a little more time for studying.

Allen made notes and put them back in our secret hiding place before the others came back into the cell from their outside activity. We could have gone that last hour, but Allen figured it's more important and imperative to study. So Allen used another big word. I didn't understand, and he tried to explain it gets more important for now, but it was hard for me to understand those big words. And I still couldn't put it all together about sexual stuff. But Allen insisted that it will all come to me. I just have to be patient, and I was mow able to understand that word, and knew what that word meant.

Patrick, Bernard, Billy, David, were all playing cards and asked Alan. If we wanted to play sex handed smear and Allen said, "Yes we can take a break from our studies. So we all played cards," Patrick said, "Did you hear about the almost break out in cellblock M. some men dug through the wall and crossed over to the cellblock N. And no way out from their but that only means more checkups and more inspections for the rest of us." But trying to escape as a prisoner last hope and escapes are planned by desperate men, and most prisoners try at one time or other to escape.

But most plans for breakouts are discovered, long before they are executed, and all they prove is just added checkups and more punishment. But then again, what is life without some Rae of hope, and there will always be someone making new plans and think he can come up with the perfect plan for escape, and some risk it all on one hope and finding some desperate men comes up with him this perfect plan for a breakout to freedom. This is their final hope and they even talk other men with lesser sentences to join them and their easily convinced to go along with the plan. We never discussed anything like that in our cell, because we had our own hopes and dreams also.

The next day we heard all about the prison break, and they just got as far as of next cellblock. Not very far more than anyone, but we all paid the price for their trial escape, only got two more checks and 24 hours, and three hours after lights out. But then every once in awhile someone does make that final escape to the outside, but most get caught and are brought right back for more punishment.

But there was one man from this prison system. That was never found, and his name is enshrined among the prison system and his name was Mark Stilwell. About 30 years ago time in four other man-made prison break. The only one that was never brought back was Mark Stilwell. They thought that he died in the swamp; some say that he got killed by reptiles, but it still remains a mystery today and it gives some desperate man that final hope. They need of making it on the outside. And you can't take that away from anyone that final little bit of hope is where you find it. Lights were dimming, and the six of us in cell 172. Quickly got ready for bed. We still had our good cell record to uphold and to protect and wanted very much to keep that rating.

September 17, 1981 breakfast march this morning seemed louder than usual? And with the crashing of bars with the guards yelling, sometimes enough to break your ear drums. After we had a fair breakfast. We had two hours of work detail, and then our one and a half hour out side activity. A softball game, for some of us cons, others have other recreational activity or just sat and watched and didn't participate. Up until noon lunch and then back to ourselves to do whatever we wanted to do for the day. Some went to the library, some went to study in there cell's, some went to work, and others had visitors.

Allen and me of course, we were going to get back at our studying. Allen said, "I was doing very well, but it still would take a lot more time to get me that eighth grade diploma, and to gather all evidence needed to turn the odds in our favor, and to gather the right people that we can trust." And Allen said, "I think I can trust this new young intern Jesse Wright. That works in our infirmary, he seemed like a trusting person, and I'm going to bait him to find out if I can trust him. The only thing I ask him so far was questions about sex organisms and the malfunctioning of hormones. He seemed well educated along that line in that subject, and then I ask him more questions. Next time I see him."

And especially I'm going to ask him if he will examine you physically, and make a record of his findings and not turned over to the prison system. But to do it in secret for us to help us prove your case against the District Attorney of your county, until were ready to make our move. We need more time to investigate that District Attorney, and that Sheriff's Department as well. And also that so-called laboratory.

Once we get our investigations made and some evidence and can help prove your case. Then and only then will make our move. If I get my proof positive first. I'll have to go with my case first. Okay for you and I said, "You're the boss", and we finished putting our stuff away just before lights out, we both put in a full day and sleep comes very easy. Because of that tired feeling very tired, in fact, if we didn't have our studying this stuff to do. Like other programmers a lay down during the daytime.

Morning brought a new day, September 24, 1981. James is in his first year now of imprisonment. The people in his town have probably all forgot about James L Lundgrenn, so we'll wake them up some day, I promised you James Allen said, "And when we do make enough noise they will wake up." Maybe the entire state. Maybe we'll even make national news for our efforts." Allen also said, "I got one visit coming up with Bob Bailey early October. In fact, just two weeks, and he'll come and see you also will because he is all set up for your visitation with you as your only cousin and will see what he is found out next month, on my case, especially.

He has to link this guy with my dead girlfriend Sandy, if Bob can match up the blood, semen taken from Sandy's body. Bob told me that he is going to get this man's blood type, one way or the other, without him knowing it. And if it matches then and only then, we can get a court order to make him give a sample for testing

And then we got them pined, I'll have enough evidence to overturn my conviction, and my freedom, And I want to get my law degree with the state of Georgia, but that won't slow down the work on your case. And we can almost proof already that you are incapable of doing rape and thus there would be no motive to murder that 12-year-old girl and get your case over turned on that basis alone.

So James, give it some thought of what you plan to do on the outside for you and your mom. Education is the answer, but you can take night courses and work maybe as a painter Patrick said you were doing fine. And he was teaching you the fundamentals about painting, and he said you did real fine on the cellblock that you painted a while back, sure it's a job and a better than shoveling cow manure or and smells a hell of a lot better so give it some good thought for your future James.

October 8, 1981. Its visitor's day for Allen. I know he was looking forward to this visit at 2 p.m. this afternoon and maybe Bob will have some good news to help his case so I get into my studying all afternoon. I was in the cell all by myself and at 3:30 p.m. Allen came back from his visit with Bob. But he was not too excited, and that meant nothing new.

I immediately ask him how things went and he replied, nothing different than I knew last time, but he did get that blood test. From that man, he said he was going to get secretly. Just how he got it was very tricky, said he got in a fight with the guy in a bar, and got some of his blood on his handkerchief. Later had analyzed and had typed up as the B. plus, positive. Just a little different than Sandy's, but enough to make a different blood type and the laboratory and evidence that was gathered at the crime scene and the sperm analysis. And of course that will only prove that he had sex with her that night.

Yet Bob was hopeful that in two weeks, when he comes back to see you that he would know more about that blood work, but nothing new for your case, James he said.

Away, we got back to our schoolwork, and Allen said, "Tomorrow I'm going to see that man that works in the infirmary, Jesse Wright and see if he wants to help us in a very special way and secrecy."

The supper bell rang loud and clear, and after supper we still had another hour and a half before lights out. Again tomorrow is another new day, and after breakfast, Allen told Pat to keep a lookout for me and went to meet Jesse at the infirmary. And I was told later how that meeting went. Allen said, "James when a convict is not guilty. And he needs very special help, and not many people around the prison system are willing to give that help to a convict. And I wondered if you were the type of first and that could and would help a convict. In his hour of need and that a man could trust, all the way. I haven't got much to pay you, but I am studying to be a good Attorney. When I get out of here, I will try to pass my law degree that may be a man like me could trust you enough to confide in you.

And I plan on being a very good Attorney. After I get out on the outside. And maybe there's something. I'll be able to do for you, when the time comes, and Jesse said, "Well. That's just great. And yes, I would be that type of person to help you in your hour of need. And you can trust me."

And Allen said, "We have to hide our findings and tell we are ready to use them and hidden from the prison system." Jesse thought for a moment and said, "OK. I got just a place to hide things." And Allen said, "I want you to make an examination of one of my friends in cellblock D. James L. Lundgren. He has a very special problem. In his lower track of his buddy, and we can compare notes after you make your examination, and then make our files, and I am okay" when can you see him and how can we arrange it. Jesse said, "Tell James that I half to recheck is nose that was broke a while back. I was a guy that set it for him. Remember let's go for next Wednesday at 2 p.m. okay and Allen said, "I'll bring him to the dispensary myself."

So later Alan told me all about, what happened and my appointment to see Jessie at 2 p.m. on Wednesday. And I ask if there was anything I had to know or to do. And Allen said, "No just be there and I'll talk to Jesse after he looks at you and makes his examination." He left the questions, be prepared to tell him about your childhood diseases like you told me, and tell him everything you remember from that experience.

So naturally I was very excited about Wednesday, and what the day would bring. And so was Allen of chorus so after lunch, we compared notes for Wednesday and Wednesday after lunch. Allen went with me to the infirmary for my nose examination. Allen waited in the waiting room, and Jesse said, "I should strip all my clothes off and were this white smock and checked my nose first that he looked at my rear end and then my front end and felt each testicle. And then tried to strip the skin on my penis, backward and could not go so and remarked, well. It looks like Alan suggested the right thing.

You say you had the mumps, and when you were about 10 or 11 years old. I said, "My Ma rapped very hot flax seed between my legs. Jesse said, "Well that will bring down the swelling, but the damage was already done and permanently. I'll risk my entire life and career that you cannot get an erection no matter how hard you tried," and he called Allen into the room, so we can discuss our findings and make our files and hide them for future use, when Allen came in, they talked in language, I did not understand and Jesse said, "When the time comes, we can get this to the Governor for an immediate overturn of James's conviction." But then you'll still have to deal with the county, and they could be a problem. So we need something to prove that they did not make a thorough investigation of James's case."

We need some witnesses, and James was examined in the lab didn't make a physical examination of him and looked at his sex organs and the lower part of his body, but must have destroyed the evidence of those findings. Allen asked me if I remembered that examination, and we'll get it and I replied yes. Dr. Van something is all I remember young fellow a few years older than I was. Allen said, "At the end of October. I got Bob coming to see James, and he'll get that information for us and Jesse can pass along the information to Bob."

Jesse said, "One more important thing. He got out his camera and said this is a very important camera has a microscope and he took pictures of James's genitals and face for identification and very close ups of the genitals that you could see they were crushed on James's penis." And added this will be our proof positive. As soon as you can get more evidence on that laboratory and that crooked DA's office. And don't forget that Sheriff's office either.

CHAPTER 6

New Discoveries
About James

So okay you guys get James dressed and go back to your cells and I'll take care of the files. Allen and I felt very pleased as we walked back to cellblock, and joined up with the rest of our crew and maybe play some cards for changes. We need a break form our studies anyway. And remember James not a word to anyone, okay, okay I said.

At the end of October, I had my visit with Bob and he didn't have much of anything to tell us and could see one of us next month, but not both. But they would let me know for sure, but he did say that young intern at the laboratory was let go for an undisclosed reason, but he got a line on where he went to, and also had one interview with him.

Bob said, "I told him I was writing a book, and wanted information on James L. Lundgren. I was interested in writing his story. And he was very glad to help, but he got red in the face when I ask him if he had made an examination of James's lower part of his body to determine if in fact. You're the man that raped that 12-year-old girl he got all read in the face and clammed up tight. But I think under pressure, he will crack, and when the time comes, he will tell us the true facts, at least I am hoping."

So I relayed everything that Bob told me to Allen, and he said, "Maybe we can get this done sooner than I thought with a little good luck, we can maybe get you out of here sooner than expected to get you out of this hellhole and back to your mom, now I had tears in my eyes crying like a little boy, and Allen was holding me tight like a father would hold his son was like a great comfort.

Well a few months have passed, very quickly and were getting close to Christmas time. And we had no word from Bob at all. And we wondered what happened to him. But just a few days before Christmas. A letter came for Allen from Bob. Most of it was in code for Allen to figure out later, but Bob said he was sick with pneumonia for six weeks, and almost didn't make it. And Allen said, "That's all we need yet is bad luck. It's just another setback, but then, there's always the unexpected", and he said he will get back to see us the middle of January, but nothing else knew, for now. We'll see you on the 14th of January, James and instead of Allen I. couldn't arrange a visit with him.

Allen said, "Don't worry. I did plan on the few setbacks. It just takes a little more time; he assured me that the setbacks happen all the time." So we got to look forward to seeing Bob in January 14, 1982. Other than that it's back to the usual daily routine for Christmas. We all got a movie in the mess hall. It was a Western by John Wayne called Sons of Kate Elder. Once in awhile, we do get a movie for good behavior, but then and only then.

Allen said, "I should read a lot, and we do get newspapers and magazines from the outside and world events, so I am getting smarter all the time at least Allen told me so. Can anyone believe I am the same man that came here, 17 months ago? But one year in a place like this is like an eternity seemed like a lifetime, even one week seems endless January snow came and on warmer days. We made snowman in the yard and the usual snowball fights were sometimes fun. When I got hit with a hard snowball in the nose, and it hurt like crazy, so Allen took me to the infirmary.

And a male nurse said it was easy to re break your nose. Those membranes can get rebroken easily takes a long time to heal completely up. I ask him were Jesse was and he said that young fellow got transferred out to another prison system. Allen was very surprised, and I was also Allen ask if he left any notes or letters for him. The intern said nothing. But I can find out where he is if it's important for you to know. Or maybe get his address, and you can write him. I guess it wouldn't be against the prison regulations if I did that. I should know by next time James comes in with his nose in two weeks, so check with me then okay.

So on the walk back to our cells, Allen, said another big disappointment, another big setback for us and we were both very disappointed by this new development. But Allen said, "We'll have to start over this male nurse seemed like a friendly enough person. If we could get a doctor to make those examinations on report and signed and sealed by the infirmary. But then every single thing was through the warden and you and I know he isn't willing to help us.

Now, January 15, 1982 Allen said, "It's a matter of testing, and if there is nothing to test no case. James looked kind of like he didn't understand so I'll explain it again in a little more detail. Take your testicles, for example, you can not get an erection to produce a sperm, and no sperm, means there isn't nothing to test. So no case, just the simple fact to take sperm and the Genesis does the words they use in such testing process, so I think of a sample from that little 12 year old girl that was raped. They had to save a seaman sample for testing, and there would have been seaman in her vagina. And then they need to find a match to that seaman and the only way to do that is to get a sample from a suspect. Were they needed a blood type, and they also need the sperm sample. And those so-called lab technicians, who knew that very fact. At least they were supposed to have known that or save the sample from that girl. Then in fact, they would just be matching up blood. And that's not enough in a rape case.

Knowing that you are an O positive blood type, and the girl was an O positive that's the most common blood type that there is, but it's not conclusive enough for 100% proof positive. Any Attorney that's worth anything could have made a case against such evidence to send a man to death or life in imprisonment. You have to have that 100% proof, just matching blood type is not enough sperm on the other hand is different, and is most unmatchable.

I know you don't understand this James, but believe me. Today they have to have more evidence the get a conviction on a rape and murder case. More than just a blood type for the conviction for rape and murder, let's say for instance. The only way they can get a blood type is by taking it from your blood, form a man where everything is working normal, and they can get a seaman test through your penis and your testicles but then yours are not working normally so no sperm, no test, no rape, and surely no motive and no murder by you James. I promise you this case, we will put to the governor. When the time comes, when and only if we have to and it looks that way now and we got to get you retested. When we can arrange it with that new male nurse Tony Morrow, but he is not a doctor or an intern, but he may be able to suggest something.

Or suggest someone, because it's impossible to get it used to estimate on a quiet side in places like this prison or in regular doctor can make an examination. But then we can't be sure that he will release that evidence to the Attorney. After all, it's not his job to help convicts out of here it's taken care of them while they are here. And that is if he is inclined to help and in secret bypassed the warden, so you see James. We have a big higher hurdle to jump across, and it will take some time. My case is easier and just two more things and then ready to make my move to get out of here.

Pat promised me he would look out for you, after I am gone, James said, "I'll be lost without you Allen, and I was now crying very hard, Allen put his arm around me and gave me comfort again like a father, would his son and said, "Well in a few days I'll be seeing Bob, and maybe he'll have something new to add to our situation on January 14, when he comes I'm going to give him some instructions of seeing a doctor specialists, on sperm and Genesis; and all the childhood diseases, that you got when you was just a kid and get that all analyzed for us and to see your mother and see what she remembers about your childhood mumps. She will remember something I'm sure.

I remember telling Allen that my mother didn't know any more than I do about what you call sexual things and Allen said, "Bob will know how to handle it. So don't worry. Today is January 12, Monday, and in two days I will see Bob, so you just keep up your studies James," he also said photographs would be helpful and if Jesse didn't lose those test papers that he took with him. And if we can find him? Ill give Bob is full name and places where he can look for him.

I'll offered Bob a full-time job and investigator in my firm, when I get out of here and he will be my chief investigator, and Attorneys need a lot of investigating work to be done so he is willing to help us in any way. It is almost impossible to smuggle in a camera in to a place like this. And they do make them very small nowadays, the size of a fountain pen. For instance and you're allowed to have lead pencils to do our writing, not the ink type. And if he did find something that small, maybe it would be possible. The lights were dimming, which meant the end of another day;

we all scramble to get into bed. And I scratched off in other day on our calendar. January 12, 1982.

So the two days past, and Wednesday was here after noon lunch Allen sent me to see Bob, in the visitors room an awful lot on my mind to remember what to tell him. And I had been numbered from one to six. I got to the visiting a half hours early, and waited just in case he would be early, and he was, after the usual greetings and I told him everything Alan wanted me to. And he told me the farmer called me and said, "His oldest son Fred Baines was the one I talked to at the farm that day and marked it down in his books. The date and the time and told you to come back in two weeks, so now your story is corroborated. Your statement that you gave the police that day, and he sent me a signed statement to that effect. So I'm building a complete file, and I sure will see those specialists. Allen wanted me to see, and as far as his cases concern, there is nothing.

Nothing new to add and I can see him in two weeks. The third of February and I'll look up that Jesse Wright shouldn't be hard to trace a prison Dr. Intern. But that camera will be the most difficult. So don't count on it and tell Allen for a Governor to overturn an execution. He needs probable causes, but for a life sentence, he needs more proof than that so there is a difference. And you're on the right track, as far as the district Attorney is concerned. I only got he was up for election, when I found that young officer, and he made a slip of the tongue. A few days ago, when he said, "He was ordered not to look at the other suspect. And then he had red in the face and quickly shut his mouth.

He knew that he said something important. And I acted like it didn't matter that there was a connection between the District Attorney; and the Sheriff's Department; to desist the investigation, and it had to come from the District Attorney's office. Maybe they didn't know there was anything from the lab department that remains to be Sean. And maybe they had known that such evidence might have been destroyed or lost whatever. So are visiting time was over, and I said goodbye to a new friend and went back to my cell, where Allen awaited my return, anxiously I quickly told them everything that Bob told me witch wasn't a lot and Allen said, "Well, you got one more piece of your puzzle and a signed statement is good in any court. When you consider the time factor.

And that time factor is you who said you left home at 9:00 a.m. 35

minute bicycle ride to the farm, giving you 15 minutes to talk to the farmer another 30 minutes to paddle your bicycle to the scene of the crime. He wasn't sure about that time, because you have no watch to keep time. So I had to be 10:30 a.m. and the corner, placed the time of death. Around 9:15 a.m. July 6, 1979. So that farmer just gave you an important alibi, and with all this evidence they couldn't have sent you here in the first place.

If they would have did their jobs correctly, because they didn't talk to everyone at that farm." I finally said, "Bob sends his best to you, and he looked pretty good for being very sick and almost died," Allen said, "We better go to the yard now for a few hours." I got a guy in the yard, I want to see he is a camera expert, was it his business on the outside before he got in trouble with the law and wound up here. If he can smuggle me in a camera, and I'll find that out why you join the boys for a softball game. Okay."

So once in a yard Allen found his cameraman Fred Ellis, and I played ball with the boys, and then we went directly to the supper, and then back to our cell, and we couldn't talk much at that time with everyone in the cell together so would have to wait to see what Allen found out about the camera.

Allen wrote me a note and passed it to me, while the others were playing cards. We studied, and I read the note and said, I found a way to explain later. But today there may not be a later and just before bedtime, Allen said, "Fred Ellis is going to get us a camera so we can take our pitchers, and the best place to do it would be right in the infirmary. If Mr. Tony Marrow is ready to help us and we can send a negative to Bob, if we get it done by the next time he comes end of February, may be the 24th or around that time."

And I'll convey that to Bob myself, and James. You have to realize the importance of taking these pictures of your penis and testicles is in upsetting thing, but it has to be done. I said, "OK don't worry. I'll do whatever you say, I have to do, and Allen said he talked to that male nurse. This morning, and he ask if you could come in so he could look at your nose, and he ask if I could come with you and we'll talk to him more about your case. I asked one of the guards, if I could go with you, because I didn't want someone to break your nose again.

So at the infirmary, Tony first looked at James's nose and then Allen talked to him and said, "Tony, what do you know about hormones glandular or malfunctions and childhood diseases like mumps and rickets." I was lost with this kind of talk, and Tony said, "Not a lot," Mr. Tony Morrow. Let me tell you about this book. I got it from the doctor, a couple months back, and if you read this book. It will enlighten you of such problems, let me tell you what I'm talking about thousands of people over United States suffer from some kind of thyroid problems, grandeur malfunctions would other glam problems that clause sleep disorders, anxieties sexual malfunction, depressions. And slow down sexual activity, all are caused by childhood diseases.

Do you know that 15% of the male population and United States suffer from some form of a lack of sexual activity, and that mumps rupture in the testicles stunt the growth of sexual organisms that whatever size penis. A boy at 10 years old has it never gets any bigger. It also causes a hormonal malfunction that grows hair on the chest or whiskers on the face or hair on the sex organ itself.

All these things are in the book." Tony said, "Well, what the hell you are getting at," Allen said, "I'll tell you what I'm getting at and that is, if you are willing to help us, what numbers your level of training is now, your former comrade at work here. Was going to help us, but got transferred out to another Prison. And after you read this book. We would like to know if you will be willing to help us with my friend James's problem. Because he could not have raped that 12 year-old girl, for any girl for that matter.

He was then, on July 6, 1979 incapable and still is of doing anything sexual, because he cannot get an erection caused by childhood illness called mumps, and he was wrongfully charged and convicted and sent here for a brutal crime he did not commit. He could physically not have been able to do it, and thus I say to you, Tony Morrow read that book and then ask yourself if you're willing to help us in a secret way do you realize there are more homosexual's today than ever. And those are also closed by glandular malfunctions, problems caused from childhood illness and even too much coffee can slow down the sexual activity of a normal male." Tony Morrow said I must have missed a lot in med school. And thank you for the education, and I'll let you know in a few weeks, and I will consider helping you.

Allen said as we left the infirmary. I know you didn't understand all of that James, and there's no way to explain it to you in their language that you could understand that just keep up with your book work and some day you will understand, but at least Tony got my point. And that was the most important. I said, "I didn't understand anything that you said.

Now we were back in our cell, and we can study till suppertime. The rest of our crew is in the yard outside now February 1. Bob would be here to see us in two day's this time Allen would see him and Allen was hopefully would know more about Fred Ellis, and that small camera. He said would be here in a few days, probably by the 10th of February or so. And if Tony will help we can send that entire camera back with Bob at the end of the month. And if not he can still make his investigations and find that guy Jesse Wright and me alone at this time. When I see them so we had a lot to look forward to in the next few weeks. So James keep up what your studies, that is the key for you, and the future.

And if we get you to that eighth-grade level, you can easily get your diploma on the outside and then take your home courses or classes at the community center, and you'll be able to get a better job to help support your mother, and very especially there is help available for your problem with an operation on your penis. It's not even that painful, they just freeze and clip off the end like a regular circumcised, that they do now on all male babies when they're born. The doctor just does it at birth as a regular practice lights went out ending another day.

February 3, 1982 at 2 p.m. today, Bob will be here, and Allen said Pat will look out for you while I'm gone. OK Pat said don't worry. I'll take care of your boy, Mr. Attorney, so we went for two hours of outside activity, and Allen was off to the visitor's room. And I was rushed mostly waiting his return. Allen came back at 330 p.m. Went directly to the yard and asked Fred Ellis, see if he had any news about the camera? and Fred said yes. It just came this morning, and he showed me how to work that miniaturized camera. It takes 36 pitchers, and it's all set to go. I said, "I would like to make these pitchers in the infirmary. If? Tony is willing to help and to do the examination at the same time that it will take two weeks to get this back to my friend Bob will be here about February 26.

So Fred gave Allen, the camera and back in our cell we put it in our safe place, behind the toilet bowl next day was Thursday the fourth of February. And after lunch, Allen told the guard. He wanted to take James up to the infirmary, and didn't want any trouble and have some one break his nose again. So the guard was willing to let me go with James. It was 1:30 p.m.

just after lunch we went back to our cell and got that camera out of our secret hiding place and went to the infirmary.

Tony was the only one there at the moment and that was good. He said for James to put this white gown on after taking off his entire close. Allen took the pictures of everything for reference, and we also made up cards showed time and place of the examination of James's penis and genitals and the more Tony looked at James's penis and ruled over the testicles while I took the pitchers for proof that this examination was taking place. And Tony said, I will help you in any way that I can and will testify to what our findings are here today. Now that I see what you told me a while back I can agree that it would be physical impossible for him to get an erection. And I did read your book, some of it that you gave me the other day, and you've given me a new outlook. And I want to go back to med school. You have shown me that I don't really know as much as I should to be working in this infirmary, in his prison system.

Allen said, "That's the key to everything is education." And my young friend here, James started with a third-grade level when he came in here, and he is now up to six grade level, and he going to finish his education when he gets out of here." So Allen took his last photographs, and we were about done in the infirmary; and ready to go back to our cellblock for last two pitchers. Tony typed up everything on paper and Allen took the last two photographs, of those papers that closed her station for today. Back in our cell we reflected on the days happenings, February 5, 1982.

CHAPTER 7

Bob Will See the Governor for New Trial for James

eb. 6 1982, the new day brings warmer weather, and while the rest of the boys were outside Allen and I had time to talk, what we didn't get said last night. Allen said, "I am sure glad that Tony is going to help us, and on the 26th of February, James. You'll have to meet with Bob and carry this camera to him. And the secret is, to not look suspicious. That is just a trick. I learned, and it's just a small fountain pen, but the point is, don't get caught. OK. And I replied, okay, but it's easier said; than done.

I would feel more comfortable if you did this, so Allen said, "Maybe there's a way, if you were sick with the flu or something, on that day and couldn't make the visit, and guard that's on duty was reasonable to let me see your visitor instead of you. I could say your relative would like to know how you are. And also a valid friend of mine and that you want me to see him for you and that just might work. So let's think about that for now, and if all goes well, we have almost enough now to present to the governor, for the new trial.

But I'll let Bob do a little more investigating in that District Attorney, and Sheriffs Department; they had to be joined together in one cause for a quick conviction; for that rape and murder case. I imagine that the news people were screaming bloody murder, and the pressure was humongous to say the least. And the victim's parents were turning on the pressure also.

And they had the suspect in jail, and the District Attorney thought who was going to care about a poor slob like James L. Lundgren.

Well somebody did care about you; Allen was the first to care. And now we got Tony and Bob and Jesse. And that farmer cared enough; to offer to help in your cause, and one more thing, Bob said he found Jesse, and he had all the paperwork with him. So he is in our corner, and eventually we'll have a lot more on our side, and if we don't get any more setbacks. We could get you a new trial by the end of 1982 or sooner. And that means we both have to keep ourselves out of trouble, and especially while in the yard will do any fighting for both of us. I explained our situation to him and he offered to help willingly, but it's best not to get into that position in the first place.

James said, "I have done those lots of times since I've been here. I'm back away from anyone that talked rough to me, and that said I should stand my ground, and maybe those thugs would respect that more, than they do. I am caught between both situations." Allen said, "Well for now, just back away and later we can teach you some sort of self defense or take a course in boxing, here in prison, but then you have to consider your nose was busted three times now, you have to think about that also, just say to that bully. My nose was busted three times already, and I don't want that busted again. And that just might be the answer, but don't count on it and get too close to that guy he is just a bully and picks on smaller people than they are."

So I am asking you James just to be careful outside in the yard, and stick next to Pat and Ben OK. So I said, "Ok. I'll do that and don't worry, I'll be careful." Well on Wednesday, February 26, Allen asked the guard, if he could take James's visitor. Because James wasn't feeling well, but not sec enough to go to the dispensary or infirmary, and the guard was inclined to say. I guess you could do that, it can't be that important to the prison, not to let you make a visit. James doesn't want to go to sick bay he's feeling stomach upset, nausea. Allen got the camera out of our hiding place and was on his way to the visitor section. While I played sec and could do my studies. And the rest of the crew was outside in the yard, usually after lunch, and by 3 p.m. Allen was back and said Mission accomplished; camera is on the way to be developed. Bob found a Laboratory, that would make the examination; of the photographs. And the blood sample I sent them that we took from you in the infirmary, a few weeks ago in that little tube.

I sent that all along with Bob, and if I was now on the outside I could speed things up, a great deal in our cases, but from inside here that it's going to take some more time and things move slowly, when you're in the prison system. I would say right now, I have enough proof in your case to prove beyond a reasonable doubt that you did not commit rape and murder of this little 12-year-old girl.

And surely enough to get a governor's, maybe even pardoned. And surely enough for a Governor's new trial, and once that happens, it moves very fast, and I presume its incumbent upon all law systems, that maybe want to make the evidence disappear, so it doesn't make them look bad in the eyes of the public. But then there isn't much evidence to hide In the first place. So if there's nothing to destroy; they may put the blame on that lab technician. That was replaced. So that the District Attorney, would be cleared of any wrongdoing, but he had two order the Sheriff to desist in the investigation.

And that lab technician, that was replaced that made a slept all of the tongue. When he knew he was on tape recording, while Bob was interviewing him. And in court he will have to tell the truth. Bob hired an Attorney on the outside knows all about your case and is all set to go. I told Bob a month ago to see that Attorney from my town to handle your case for me. And I would think would in three months by May or June, for sure, we should be ready to make a visit to the Governor's mansion, to present our cases for a retrial or a pardon. Which ever the Governor is inclined to offer? If the Governor and that District Attorney, want to avoid a public scandal; that Governor may just pardon you, clearing your name of any crime.

Unless we get a major setback, let's pray all things will go well for the next 60 days. Bob sends his best grads and sorry you are sick and he also added that the camera was the best idea that we came up with for your case.

Pat and the rest of the guys came in from outside activity, and soon it would be suppertime. And in a few minutes, the loud crash of cells opening and closing and the guards yelling, shouting the top of their lungs and footsteps marching down the long corridors to the mess hall. For supper, we had hamburgers in gravy, mashed potatoes, red and green beans and coffee or milk or tea, hot or cold. A very healthful supper it was.

Ever since the early 1960s, most prisons are giving the prisoners a better diet supplement food to eat, because the present systems learned a lot about diet that help the prisoners were easier to manage than people that were malnourished. And that's feeding prisoners in better food, became part of the present system. In one of the present systems, one inmate was put in the hole for three consecutive 30 days in the hole for punishment. So he was placed on bread and water for 90 days in the hole with no lights just a toilet bowl and a mat to sleep on, and when they took him out. His fingernails grew 1 1/4 inches long. His toenails grew 2 inches long. The rest of his body was just skin and bones and was barely alive.

He looked like some of the war prisoners. When the US forces raided the island of Batan during World War II, and the Philippine islands, and the well-known death march sponsored by the Japanese. Those soldiers had to endure years of almost starvation, and most perished from the lack of nourishing food and some died of diarrhea, those are cruel and harsh punishments for any man to endure for long periods of time.

But we were not treated that way here, but they still have the 30 days in the hole. But they do feed them. More than just bread and water, at least in this prison system. Anyway I think it's all the US prison systems. I'm not 100% sure about that and some of them can dish out some kind of harsh punishments. But 30 days in the hole is the most a person has to endure, but not 60 days in a raw, that's cruel punishment. But that prisoner, probably pulled a knife and cut somebody, maybe even killed somebody in the process. So sometimes it's justly deserved, and then some prison systems are run by wardens with too much political power.

When a warden has such political power. He can make any inspections at well, any time he feels like. And if he is a cruel man by nature, and then he will express that cruel nature to the prisoners. From time to time. I have to say that we had a fairly good warden, in this prison system. So that attitude of all your inmates show is a good level of behavior, and then the hate level is low; and thus their less violence among the prisoners. And there's less chance that the prisoners will rebel against the warden if the warden is a good-natured man, and doesn't enforce his own political power. And within the prison system, there is always things going on, especially when new prisoners arrive. It takes a while for them to make an adjustment to prison life.

And it takes time to make those adjustments, but just think five or 600, men in the yard at one time; some of them are hardened criminals. Men that really have committed murder and rape, robbery and a number of crimes against society, and those men are easily provoked. And some need no provoking at all. Allen always cautions James when he goes outside to not go near those hardened criminals. Just stay away from them is the answer and stay close to Patrick and Bernard, when in the yard.

First week in March, and Bob will be there on Wednesday the 13th of March and maybe he will bring us new Hope, who are James and Alan and that is just what we look forward to this time it will be Alan's turn to meet Bob, at 2 p.m. and see what he has new to brings us this time.

Allen talked with that male nurse Tony just yesterday he had a sliver in his hand and needed to go to the infirmary to get it out and get it lanced. My guess is the word by Tony and Tony said he was still glad to help us and be on our side, but couldn't show it while he is here that when it comes time to testify. We had to served him a summons or you couldn't just go on his own that he would testify to the facts that he was part of that examination of James's testicles and penis, which are shown clearly on the photographs, and then he was still willing to help us, but not incriminate himself.

March 13, came and Alan went to the visitors section at 1:30 p.m. Bob was expected by 2 p.m. and I stayed in our cell and did some studying, while Pat and the rest of the guys were outside, and I was waiting patiently for Allen's return. And when he returned at 3:30 p.m. we had 30 minutes to gather before the rest of the crew came back. And Allen said Bob had good news, but not a lot of news, he said he talked to a young police officer, who voluntarily said, "They had another suspect at the time. James was in their jail, another suspect they were looking at, that they had probable cause to consider him as a suspect. And then all of a sudden, they made the arrest of James and Allen wondered why they did that so suddenly.

Bob said, "I think this young officer didn't know anything about the case being ordered to do a desist by the District Attorney's office. And he knew he was on audiotape, because I told them I was writing a book about that case, and adding the two slips made by two different people, should be cause to make me think they knew more than they was telling? I was recording, these conversations at the time for writing a book, and they were willing to talk while on recorder and said on tape, this statement. So that's good for our case, when the time comes.

Just when I can get to see the Governor about this a matter, I'll be working on the next couple of weeks, maybe even two months, but it shouldn't be more than another 60 days. And if it goes to trial and it will take a little longer than if the Governor just decides to pardon. James and of course there will be a lot of publicity involved. And I will try to get a change of venue, if it goes to trial because of that newest pressure and if they get James locked up in their jail, who knows how they may treat him. I thought we would go for Allen's County, which is in Columbus County.

And that's only 10 miles away from this prison. Where the trial could be held and the judge would be Marvin A. Weber and he apparently is a fairly good judge to deal with. If we draw him for the case. I also found out the other suspects, name and he was 19-year-old William B. Walker. That was to people that said there was another suspect during my interview is at the Sheriff's Department on tape, but they didn't say the name of the suspect.

Then I got lucky. When I went to lunch at the restaurant. There was a man sitting next to me when I said I was interested in the case of James Lundgren and he said yeah, there were two men, suspect's in that case, and he said Billy B. Walker, 19 years all, and he thought that James was railroaded into prison by a corrupt, District Attorney.

Now you got four people in your own hometown that thinks you didn't do it and that's a good start. Bob recapped the evidence in your case, quickly which wasn't much, you're peddling your bike down the road, stumbled onto a body lying beside the road. You kneel down to check to see if the person is alive and get blood on your close. The most natural thing for anyone to do. You call the police, which is your duty to do the police think you are the suspect. And when your story didn't check out at the farm, and now that it is corroborated by the farmer.

And shabby investigation by the laboratory, and no testing of any kind, other than your blood sample there was no effort taking, no sperm in the genesis, no examination of your testicles. By that laboratory now your camera photographs are perfect to prove your case for any Attorney.

Bob said, "Our Attorney" said, "He had more than enough evidence to overturn your conviction; was any judge without a jury trial, like the last time" and said, "That Sheriff's Department just made a rush to judgment. And so did the District Attorney office," whether they ordered a desist will be yet to prove what they didn't have any witnesses of any kind. Just circumstantial evidence that they didn't believe your story and didn't spend any time asking all the people that worked on that farm, which were four of the family members.

And they had a poor wretch, young man with a third-grade level of education locked up in jail and a thug who would care about such a person last thing Bob said was first week in June, and not to worry. But of course, we here in this prison do worry from day to day weather today is going to be that day, someone in a yard decides to knife someone standing beside you, which gets you in trouble also. Even though you were not involved. While the other men, were coming back, from the out side activity now. And we put our stuff away in our secret hiding place, and the supper bell will soon ring in half an hour or so.

I said, "To Alan for some reason, I am very hungry tonight for not doing any physical work all day and I give everyone a big smile and a thank you for there patents for helping me the last two and half years". I said, "If I get out of here I sure will come back to visit you all." All the cells opened and we went to supper, and tonight we had a speech by the warden, and we had baked ham, minced beans, grits and mashed potatoes and gravy, two kinds of vegetables, a dam good meal.

The warden gave us all a good speech about behavior, and he complimented all of us for that behavior, and for your new prisoners. That just arrived today. I say to you will follow the advice of your elder comrades, and they will guide you and help make the transition into prison life for all of you are joining cellblock D. and they have a best record for performance for two years in a row. Also performance for no trouble and less fights and just good behavior, and for that behavior, we will have a movie tonight. For those of you that want to watch and stay after supper.

And a movie tonight will be another Western by James Stewart, called Bend in the River Allen said, "Let's watch the movie and take a break from our studies." I replied, okay. And I could never afford to see a movie when

I was home. My mother barely got enough to pay their rent and food. Sometimes I earn some extra money to buy clothes and other stuff like that. And she is on my mind tonight, and maybe the movie will set my mind at ease, and maybe it's just what I need for now.

Allen old friend and Attorney I kid you said I was making a joke. And he accepted it that way, and we went on with our eating. And while we were eating. They were setting up the projector for the movie expected time was hour and 45 minutes for the movie till it was over and just about dark outside and that to our cells. We played six handed smear is the name of the game for matches, Alan and I didn't smoke but Patrick chewed tobacco and three of the others smoked cigarettes, so lights dimmed, meaning lights out in 15 minutes.

Allen and I put our stuff away, and we all were in our bunks, settled in for the night as the guard walked by to make his inspection that we were all in our bunks. I felt tired for some reason, and Allen felt a lot of different emotions. He felt gallant for doing a good job. His first and most precious job. He felt proud, and everything was overwhelming, as he laid there in his bunk and whispered a good night to me.

All those feelings, Allen was feeling at the moment. And I laid there for 15 or 20 minutes and couldn't sleep and I also was feeling very homesick and missed my mother dearly and I said good night to Alan. My friend my comrade and my Attorney. And he said. Likewise, as another day ended your sell 172, cellblock D. As and marked the page from the calendar March 14, 1982.

CHAPTER 8

Bob Phoned
the Governor

March 15, 1982. Although we don't have any plans for the next two weeks, it's just ordinary daily routine and a trip to boredom sometimes. But one only gets time to reflect on our cases, and study all the extra hours we can possibly get. Allen gets at his law books, and I get back to my sixth-grade studies. So I got a long way to go too get to the eight grades. And no way to take that final examination test. But Allen said, "He would give me a straight test, when the time comes. When his case seems to be bogged down, although Bob, is investigating this other character. But he can't prove that he was there. At that might of the murder, and the only one way to get a court order is to convince the Governor. You got wrongfully put in prison, and if you can do that. You can demand a new trial, and then your Attorney can use this other character to prove reasonable doubt. And then get your case overturned.

But my case is going well and I could be out of here in 60 days or less. Bob thought June 14 maybe or sooner, so it looks hopeful anyway. And every day that goes by without any incidences is a good day. And there seems to be just that a lot of good days with no trouble. Wouldn't it be wonderful, if just feeding us good meals was the cause for this good behavior? I'm no expert and cannot prove what I say, but it makes sense that a well fed the healthy body is a well fed, working brain, which provokes prisoners into bad behavior or can't make logical judgments about their own behavior.

But then I can't make that judgment, but Allen thinks that it's a good start for the prison, and systems, to think how they been treating prisoners. That just might be the key question? Another day goes by, and lights out in hall ways. Allen crosses off another day on the calendar. And we were all snug in our bunks by time the guard walked by our cell. With just his cane tapping on the bars, and then all is quiet until the guard makes his rounds in three hours and then again at 3 a.m. in the morning. Tomorrow is March 15, 1982. It's almost 3 years since I came here, and I'm not the same man, I was on that day. I guess I was just lucky, when I met Allen for the first time.

And maybe I'll be out of here three months before that three-year date August 22, 1979. Hopefully I won't be here by then. March 16th and 17th were just ordinary days Saturday on the 18th. We had another movie and other Western by Robert Taylor called the law and Jake Wade. That was a good movie, but I never saw it before, nor did Allen and then back to our cell than one hour to study and then Allen crosses off another day on the calendar. Tomorrow March 19 and in a few days of Bob will be here to see me and give me the news on Wednesday. Maybe there'll be good news coming our way.

Allen taught me a lot of things since I been here, and I could not have survived without him or without his help. And God bless him for that even taught me a little religion and tomorrow will be Sunday, and I will go to church, with Alan and he taught me that I can believe in something bigger than just you and I and when I get out of here. I'm going to teach my mother, all I have learned from Allen. Maybe not everything.

But I am looking foreword to Sunday service at 9:30 a.m. only last one hour, but we sang songs, and it's just all fates put together, not just one.

But if the prisoners do not want to attend they don't have to; they don't force religion on no one. When I was nothing before I came here. I don't know what my father was or mother was, if any religion at all. At least I can't remember her going to any church. In fact, I don't know much about my mother at all. Only the thing I remember that my father ran off. When I was just eight years old or so I can harder remember what he looks like. On Monday morning after breakfast, Allen and I went to the library, and we were looking through the register file of prisoners that came and went from this prison system. And we stumbled across a name called Bill

D. Lundgrenn was year and released in April 1979, and I told Allen this could have been my father. I didn't know my father meddle initial, but it's possible this was him, I thought he was dead. And surely he doesn't deserve any respect.

And Allen said, "Just put it out of your mind and don't think about it that will be better for you. And there are people like that, they just don't care, and their children have to pay the price for their sins; and lack of understanding that being a parent is a serious responsibility, and not saying this about you James, but most of the abandoned children turn up in the prison system. At some given point in their life because of that lack of parental guidance and thus they pay this total price of the father's or mothers sins."

Well in two days Bob will be here again, and I asked Allen, what I had to tell Bob this time. Allen replied. Not much and just make sure you get his messages is the most important for today. Those two days went fast and Wednesday at 1:30 p.m. I was on my way to the visitors section to meet with Bob. I had a half an hour to wait just in case he would be early, but he came exactly on time, as usual.

And after the usual greetings, he slipped me a small note. No envelope just a small piece of paper for Alan. It was in code, but he told me the important things and he told me things looked good on my case, and he phoned the Governor of the State of Georgia and had a good conversation with him and the governor said he would see him in person on the end of April.

He said, "He told the Governor some of the things we have for the case, but not everything and I also talked to him about Allen's case, and the Governor was inclined to hear about both cases, on the end of April. And he seemed like a most reasonable man, and willing to listen to your case. And I hope I am good enough to persuade him to give you a trial or a pardon, which ever is workable, but you want to clear your name of any wrongdoing for the future, because it is important to have your name cleared of such a terrible crime.

Because without it, you are marked forever, some says that without a court trial. You can't clear your name of that charge. Allen would know more about that, than I would Bob said. "I think that very corrupted Crockett, District Attorney would rather not be humiliated." And surely that Sheriff Department would be disgraced too say the least. But as for now, they don't suspect anything that's going on, but maybe the Governor

Wanted time to check your case, and what they had a against you, so maybe they communicated.

Bob said, "But I think we have a good case and a good chance of getting you out of here by June. But there isn't much more I can do from the outside. But Allen will know what to do." Allen's case, they say that blood work was compromised, and the semen test was compromised. Also but Allen's blood was not found on the scene so with a trial I'm sure we could convince a jury, but Allen will have to do the work from the inside now. And he will know if it's possible to get a trial date.

James take this message to him, if the guard finds it, relay the message. I told you James and how everything else is that's going on, and I said, "Can you make a check up on a man named William D. Lundgrenn got out of here, April or end of March 1979. I'm not sure of the date. He was charged with rape and got five years for statutory rape. So see if you can find where he is and who he is. You check the county records in our town. So our meeting was now over and we said our final goodbyes.

And Bob said, "See you guys in two weeks; maybe have some good news by then, or both of you." So I had no trouble getting back to my cell, and Allen was patiently waiting and the others were outside in the yard playing softball. And I told Alan, everything that Bob told me, gave him the note that was in code. Of course was great news, but hopeful also the note said only two blood types were on the scene of the murder, and both blood types were different so you should be able to show cause and convince the Governor for a pardon.

But Allen said, "Hell no, I don't want no Governor's pardon. I want a trial for both of our cases. And I promise you, James we will win and make them look ridiculously bad as they are and hold them accountable for their actions; and wrongdoing. And it's up to you and me as citizens to hold them accountable; for their crimes against society and you. But then it's your decision of which way to go and a pardon does not include the clearing of your name from that crime, and that's the very point.

We have the responsibility to hold them accountable for their crimes against you, and society and they deserve the worst that can possibly happen to law enforcement personnel, jail or disbarment or both. But realistically, all we can hope for is disbarment for the District Attorney, and to have the Sheriff run out of town like to use it in the old days. But that's the best we can hope for.

March 22 night fall, and another day to cross off of the calendar, the last thing Allen said to me was. It was up to you and me to make them pay for their desisted crime. Last thing I said is your right, let's do it.

Turned the March 23. Early up for breakfast. James had to see Tony about his nose bleeding once in awhile, and Tony gave him some causes and bandages to stuff up his nose to stop the bleeding. There wasn't anything else to tell Tony except I did mention to him by June. And that was all I told him, and without any setbacks that is. It doesn't seem like much can happen at this point, but there is always the unexpected, and we hope that nothing would go wrong. The days ticked by very slowly, each day seemed like an eternity, not only for me, but for Alan as well.

But Allen said, "Keep up your fate." And I was praying on Sunday, church Allen went with me all of the time, but he was Catholic. Born and raised that way, I didn't know much about any religion, and knew very little about any religion for that matter, before I got here anyway, April 5 was now here and just seven days Bob would be here for his usual visit, and this time, he will see Allen.

Allen now had me in the seventh grade, and if I studied hard for the next two months could maybe make the eighth grade. So I am definitely not the same man who came here almost 3 years ago. I couldn't have used a word like definitely or know what it meant at that time. Allen said, "This time, I'll tell Bob, how to get you a trial date, and maybe my own as well, public opinions. Ill tell Bob to let the Governor know that we mean business. And will go public, if they will not grant us a second trial date and my cases as well as yours."

Wednesday the 12th of April. That's what I'll tell Bob, if the governor is willing to grant us a trial, and we won't go public. But the public will know anyway, but maybe he can save some of his embarrassment of bad publicity. Before his next term election, if he is bold enough to run again.

Sure they'll be willing, I'll bet and chances of change of venue for your case to Columbus County looks good. Just 10 miles away, and the district judge has power to grant such a change of venue; and Bob have most of our file already. And then will take the last pages of our file along when the time comes. And now take him what he needs on the 12th of April. But if they grant the trial here, we can get the rest of our stuff out by subpoena, and they will have to subpoena me as a witness to your case.

After all, I was the first one to discover the dysfunction nation of your sex organs. And there's one chance that I could be appointed part of your legal team and sit beside your regular Attorney, and as a witness. And we'll subpoena, Tony from the infirmary. He will be important witness for your defense. James said, "To Allen I. won't have to undress in front of the court, will I." Allen said, "No. But you will have to be examined by another laboratory here in Columbus County to verify our findings, but that will be good for our case. I'll ask for the first week in June for a trial, and I believe it will come. While we still can't be hopeful, and pray.

Also just about six weeks from now, and it takes about 30 days for the judge to grant a change of venue. So it can't possibly be before that first week in June, and a few more days, Bob will be here, and I will give him all that information and will get the ball rolling in our direction. April 9 on a Sunday after church, we reflected on our daily plans. And we made a list of things that we proved that were faults in James's case. But in three more days, Bob will be here and maybe he will know if we get a time date for the trial that will be most important for both of us, all afternoon we stayed inside the cell and study their books, while the others were playing softball outside.

I ask Alan, what he thought was going on with Bob right now, Allen said, "By now he is seeing the Governor and I think it looks hopeful is my prediction. After today there will only be two more days till Wednesday at 2 p.m. again, the usual time. But we won't get the trial date. Just now and probably but just a possible date."

Allen gave me test for the seventh grade and said for the next four weeks. I should study for an eighth grade, and he would give me another test for an eighth grade. He also said I had to make 75%. He also said he will study every available moment, when the supper bell rang and the outside inmates were already on their way down to the mess hall so the guard walked us down separately, while saying why you guys like outside activity don't, and Allen said, "I am studying to be an Attorney. And when I get out of here I'm going to sue you for damages in court," the guard gave a big laugh and said, "That's your right convict consular and gave him a push forward."

At chow, we didn't get to sit with our regular bunch Patrick and

Bernard and the guys for supper so we eat our wonderful meal. We quickly went back to our cell; we were there 10 minutes before the others arrived. And of course they want to play cards, and Allen said, "No you four guys play, we got studying to do," and James got his schoolwork class to study for an end to all words that will be lights out, and one more day to cross off of our calendar. Tuesday was a copy day of Monday and Wednesday, Allen left at 1:30 p.m. for the visitor section to meet with Bob. I had great anticipations for his return. So I just got at my studies, while Pat and the others were outside playing softball game again, and I could hardly wait for 3:30 p.m. to arrive. When Allen would be back, and at times seemed endless. And I gave a big prayer for something positive, from Bob's visit.

At 3:35 p.m. Alan walked down the long cellblock and walking on that cellblock floor. You could hear footsteps from a long way off. Footsteps making a lot of noise, even from a long way off. But when I see a great big smile. I knew that something important was about to take place. And that smile said success was here, and Allen started telling me everything that Bob said to him that Bob, in fact saw the Governor and he granted you a trial for June 1 week in Columbus County, Georgia. Just 10 miles from this place and he said the court arranged a trial for me after your case. Because I am the star witness in your case.

And we both will be transferred to Columbus County Jail, 72 hours before that date so by the eighth of June, for sure. We got just 28 days, but keep it quiet. I don't want anyone to know or some crazy inmate to feel sorry for him and take it out on us for our good fortune. Bob said, "I would get subpoenaed two weeks before that time, and another subpoena for material, and all my paperwork that I have collected over the last two and half years, but the fact is legal, together. I don't see how they could do it in the other way and also they would subpoena Tony", and Bob said, "They also sent a subpoena to Jesse and his paperwork for a witness on his examination he took two years ago.

James just keep up with the studies, for the next 28 days and I replied. I'll study, all I can and it's you and I together to put those guilty ones at least out of they're jobs. But they deserve to be sent to the penitentiary for many years, and any time, law enforcement people get in prison is many times rougher on them than it is the average criminal. We won't say nothing to Patrick and the others OK partner and I replied okay partner.

CHAPTER 9

The Governor Granted
James a Trial

Thursday, April 13, 1982, just 28 days left and will be transferred to Columbus County Jail. And maybe freedom for you James, but maybe I'll have to come back here. I'm not sure just what's going to happen. Or they could possibly keep me there those 30 days, and I would prefer staying in Columbus County ten miles, and will hope for that eventuality. Allen said, "I'll be a right by your Attorney to make sure he does his job right. After all, I still am your Attorney wanted and paid for. You remember that, don't you," I replied yes. I remember very well, I gave you $.50, and I thank you for your friendship and your help. I don't think I would have made without you. When that dinnertime bell rang out, the sex of us marched to the mess hall.

The dinner looked very good with a good portion of meat loaf, mashed potatoes and gravy, with two kinds of vegetables and coffee tea or milk or two of the kind which ever we preferred some new prisoners were present, and that meant a speech from the warden and it was his same speech as a last group, a few months back, and he gave our cellblock, the best rating of the entire prison, which meant a lot to us as a group. And you young inmates take the advice of your elders, and you'll be able to make that transition to prison life. So enjoy your meal was his last word.

He also added a well fed prisoner is a good behaving prisoner, so we eat that wonderful meal and back to our cell for more studies. While the other boys went outside for games, and Allen was studying his law books to get his possible degree but he will have to take the bar examination on the outside, but he said he felt he could easily pass that bar examination any time. But that will be a while yet, he added that he showed a lot of confidence. But I would like to be close to you, may be set up a law practice in your town and God knows your town needs a good defending Attorney. With all those crooked law enforcement people that are there, and the way they push people into jail in that community,

I said, "That would be wonderful sound like a great idea, but I can't express my feelings right at the moment." "I was crying and Allen was holding me tight like a father holds his child." As Allen said, "You are going to be OK; James I'll get you a state scholarship to go to high school first. And then collage get you the best education that US money can buy, and it won't coast you nothing, because under the false imprisonment act we'll have a good case to sue the District Attorney, and that ass hole sheriff. We'll sue for damage for false imprisonment for three years of your life may be $250,000 per year." I said, "Can we do that." Yes, we can was Allen's reply, and I'll be your Attorney for that case. And my fee will be 35%. How doze that sound, my friend.

I said, "That sounds fine to me". When the cell door opened for the return of the other cell inmates and supper would soon be ringing its bell, and then one more day would soon be over, so a good supper and back to the cell block D. So we played cards with the boys still dark and light out. Allen crossed off another day on our calendar, saying just 26 more days to go as the lights went out, we were all smuggled in our bunks.

But Allen said, one more thing, goodnight my first client, and I replied excitedly good night. My teacher, Attorney, and friend. And Allen replied, you and I James are going to make history, for the prison, and three years of good behavior, will get us a good reformed record would be good for us. Three years of excellent behavior will surely get us a good rating and that is good for us to use against the prison system, and tomorrow is Friday and Saturday in the movie day. Probably another Western, but then, I like westerns, and so do you right partner, and that was the very last word. A good night sleep. I didn't even hear the three-hour checkup or the later checkup at 3 a.m. and was up early at 6 a.m. for seven o'clock breakfast.

After breakfast, we had two hours work detail, which we didn't expect.

We were put on new work detail, and the jobs come up from time to time. Not like it was a year ago, and that only a couple days per week, two three hours at a time, but it was not hard work or backbreaking work. And we have no choice in the matter. And I guess it was part of our leadership and sell 172, in cell block D. That the other inmates follow that leadership, and we want to keep that in our favor, for the next 26 days until June 5 or six, and we should be transferred to Columbus County Jail by then, for trial.

Allen said, "He was fully prepared already, and he was well informed of my case to the other Attorney, Jack Warfield from Morgan Creek, Georgia. That was near Allen's home town, and the judge would be Stanley Jameson, had a long history on the bench of other counties before he came here 12 years ago." He was 62 years old. Allen said, "That would be very good for us. And he is a fair-minded man and judge." So James, you just keep up the studies, and after today are just 24 more days. April 20 on a Saturday and tonight there will be another movie for us. Good convicts, and it will be just after chow so we can have time to watch it and take the time out from our studies so who can work every hour or that's available to you and we should get some paperwork or subpoenas. By next week for sure, and that will make news around the prison system, and there are guys here that resent those things terribly, and take out their resentment on those that are getting out.

So all I can tell you, James is to stay in the yard in a safe place. Next to Patrick, When I'm not around, or just stay in the cell, and study all the time. But I did tell Patrick. Our plan, because he is close to us. And I trust him. And when papers come I hope we can keep it quiet.

Our movie that night was a Western was an old Western by Randolph Scott. The man behind the gun. Lasted. 1- 45 minutes. It was almost 7 p.m. by time it was over, and as we walked back to our cell and would end the day with some study work. Or we could play cards, and I thought I should keep up with his studies to lights out, ending another day, April 21, 1982 as Allen crossed off the date on our calendar.

Sunday three of us went to church, and afterwards I said, "To Allen that I felt enlightened. But I wasn't sure if that was the word," but Allen said that the word was appropriate, because that's what the words of the minister should do to a person, so I'm slowly learning more words everyday, we expect to be subpoenaed by the first week in May, and then transferred to Columbus County Jail. Once we are there, we can start our case together. And that's Allen's job, and he is welcome for work to do in just that. For his first case that he is not the real legal Attorney. But he will be in total charge of the case.

Bob will make his visit, and the first time, we will be allowed to visit him together. Allen had asked the warden, and he agreed and I guess what's going on prompted the warden to let us both go and visit with Bob. On Wednesday this week, Allen is hoping for some answers in his case. But then there isn't much he can get any way. But if they could find out why? There were three different blood types in the room, where his girlfriend Sandy was killed. And do more testing on that date would be very helpful. It was all hinged on that one of the blood types matched mine. Allen had said, maybe things would move faster if they could explain the three blood types that were in the room.

After church the guys went outside to play ball, and we were in our cell studying both for an examination. I had to pass the eighth-grade test to see what I had learned and then one more test before we get transferred out of this prison system.

The news got around the prison system fast, and by Monday, April 23 in the yard next to me was a big guy come up very fast and said, some argumentative things to me trying to pick a fight. But Patrick was close by and took the guy and shoved him aside and said, "Look here, asshole we are not getting thirty days in the hole, because you want to pick a fight." That was the end of that the guy apparently didn't want no part of big Patrick.

After the guy left I said, "Thank you Patrick once again for coming to my rescue, and he took me back to cellblock 172, and this is where I'll spend the next three weeks if just leave the cell for chow only." So Allen comeback from library and was glad I was not hurt. And he said, "Word of our getting out of here, is making the rounds among the prisoners now." And that spells danger for you and I they resent the fact that were getting out. And we can't take a chance on getting 30 days in the whole. And then missed our chance of transfer date, so it will be like walking on eggs and you don't want to break them or walking thin line.

And I guess we have to stay in the cell is the safest place for both of us. And some of the guards are just ready for us to make that final mistake, by either one of us. And I asked Patrick to stick close to both of us. And I promised him I would help him in his case so let's just get at your studies, and it will be lunch time very soon. And that's when things can go wrong. I told Patrick and Bernard to stick two in back of us and two in front. When we walked to the Chow line.

So the dinner bell rang, and the loud noise of the cells opening is almost unbearable, and off to lunch. Even the guards looked different, they and a little bit more, ordering us around seemed a bit mad at us and he was right outside our door, when the cell opened usually he is off down the hallways shouting orders.

So at lunch today we had come of the usual meals, and the usual sneers, made by other convicts and a few of them at our table. But Patrick was on our left side and Bernard was on our right side so just a few times on the other side of the table, and they joined up to our defense. From this kind of sneering and name calling, just to see if they could get us mad or upset, or even worse by throwing food at them were getting in a fight, which would mean 30 days in all in trouble with the guards.

One of the Convicts said to the guard, that I shoved my silver wear in my pockets, and of course they had to make an inspection. A body search and that meant a search of our cell later to see if they couldn't find anything at all. And we just had a search yesterday, so that's one they probably would not do that anyway that was just a guess, will lunch was over and we marched back to our cellblock. And after we got there of course Ben and Patrick and the others went outside for ballgames or exercise and they were also feeling the heat of being our cell mates and got plenty sneers from the other convicts. Sure they had to stick together while they were on the outside also for their own protection.

That is some of the worst things that go on in prisons and the guards seem to enjoy this kind of thing. And even tolerate such activity, but this warden seems to try his best to keep that kind of thing from happening. But then he can't be all over at one time. If they could just weed out the worst troublemakers. That would be doing this. But then the guards encourage that kind of activity, and that sort of thing, and they enjoy a locking someone up in a hole for 30 days, but believe me it is no fun. I was there one time, the first 90 days I was here.

Allen said, "I spent time in the hole and few years back so about 4 p.m. to guards came and made an inspection of our cell, but they just looked around, and they were now use to us being in our cell and after they left," Allen said, "Well it's getting to be a little too dangerous for us. So will have to be damn careful, so you get at your studies and let me worry about our protection and will be out of hear soon. I had told Bob that this thing could possibly happened one or both of us and to see if the judge could agree with the Governor that we were in danger here now from the other prisoners and to see if they would push up the date of transfer sooner than planned, and well by Wednesday, we will know One way or another, and it's just two more days.

We were hoping for those things should come about when it seemed like a long today's. And we were excited about that coming event and on Wednesday at 1:30 p.m. we were escorted to the visitors section to see Bob. He had a big smile on his saying so, that meant good news at least we hoped, and it was good news Bob said, "The judge said today that we can transfer you both out of hear on the 10th of May by armored car would take you both the 10 miles to Columbus County Jail.

But only the warden, was told the exact date and this could be kept a secret. But Bob had no other news about our cases, but only a nice visit for the first time all three of us together." Bob also said, "Once we get you out of hear will have more time to work on both of your cases, and maybe I can put a little pressure on the labbitory people to test those three blood samples carefully, those three blood samples were found on the scene. Three different types of blood, but that meant your blood was not found on the scene and that meant to other man were on the scene or two women or one man and one woman. It speculative, at least all the while I was looking for a man and the thought just occurred to me. Was your girlfriend Sandy may be on drugs?"

Allen said, "I really don't know that he thought about it for a long time before he answered the question. But there was a time or to; she didn't seem to be herself. And that changes of her mood." Bob said, "That changes the whole picture for motive. Maybe not a romantic interlude by buying and selling drugs, or its possible this other man had a jealous girlfriend. That did the stabbing of Sandy. So we'll have to think about it in different ways." So you two are having trouble here now and it won't be long and you'll be out of this terrible place. And finally the guard came and said our time was up. And we said our goodbyes to a good friend.

So the guy walked us back to sell 172, and we recapped what just took place and Allen said, "I'll make some notes of Sandy's actions were the two years that we was together, but it had to be just the last 10 months that I noticed some of those changes in her moods and everything about her. That seemed normal, but I never thought about drugs. Tell Bob said it this afternoon, but it would explain those mood changes. If she was somehow involved in the sale of drugs, I never saw any sign of those things that would indicate her in such actions. She was doing things that seemed normal, but then drug people can be very convincing. And they're able to hide their actions most of the time.

But then drug are high-priced, and I wondered where she got the money she wasn't making that much on her waitress job, but these drug people get you addicted to drugs, and then raise the price on you. I personally never had any one contacting me about drugs in our small town. In fact, I knew nothing of such things going on, but that underground world of drug sellers is everywhere in school systems on the streets as well, as in the schoolyard or everywhere you look. I just never thought about it."

Allen said, "I remember two blocks from Sandy's mother's house once was a drug bust about a year before we move into our own small 3 room apartment. I really wanted to get married, but she said she wanted to try living together first. And that first year wasn't all that bad was really great I thought."

I said, "What really went wrong with the two of you," Allen said, "That's a good question? I got mad at her just a few times and just over a few little things that upset me, but not enough for any worse arguments, she got mad a few times. But that night that it happened wasn't all that much just a little argument over her cat. And I am allergic to cats. She knew that. Yet she comes home with this full-grown cat. And I object it right away, and then the cat jumped up on top of the supper table and I swatted the cat with my hand. She thought I hit the cat too hard and started crying, and then she slapped me in the face. And I walked out the door and went to the neighborhood bar and stayed there till 12:30 a.m. come home and found her laying their dead. I checked her to see if her heart was beating, just like you and checked that little girl you got blood on your pants. And when I found out she was dead I called the 911 system. They said, "If she is dead call the Sheriff's Department so I did."

Allen then they came to the apartment, and after one hour of interrogation, they arrested me for murder, almost the same as your case. You might say. I remember there was upset furniture, and things scattered about the room. And there were three kinds of cigarette butts in the ashtray. It just comes back to me now and I don't smoke. But Sandy did, so she must have had a few visitors after I left. So I never thought about this before, until now after Bob triggered my memory, and now I'm starting to remember little incidences that there must have been two other people in the house. After I left and that would explain the three types of blood. The law-enforcement, said one of them could have been just cat, but they never checked to see if they cat was injured.

If they had a fight, between the three of them over something. Or if one of them gave the other, a shot of heroin, in the wrong vein. It could be blood would squirt out. Of that blood vein, thus producing enough blood on the end table by the couch and this all brought out new thoughts for my mind and better write this all down on paper and put it in our safe place, and I said to Allen, "You maybe have to look for another woman, but the definite blood type was this man that Bob found and got his blood type remember." Allen said, "New possibilities, brings up a new set of thoughts for all of these things." And Bob can check out this character's connections. And maybe there was no romantic involvement at all and no connection to the murder for a romantic situation.

Now the boys come in from the outside, and Pat said, "They got in a fight outside, but the guard said there was no harm done. So it wasn't a big enough deal to send us to the hole for 30 days. So, the supper bell rang loud and clear, and we were just about half way down to the mess hall was a flight of stairs leading downward. And some convict push James outline, and he fell down. That flight of stairs and got his nose broke again. I asked the guard, if I could take him to the infirmary. And while they reset his nose, must be the fourth time. The guard called the warden and told him that James broke ranks and tried to run down the stairs and I quickly said. Somebody pushed him.

I also told them the name of the young convict. His name was Ted. He was just one of the new prisoners, and James was pushed out of line. By this guy and fell down that flight of stairs shown no punishment was ordered by the warden for James. But he did order punishment for Ted got 30 days in a hole. Allen asked the warden, if there was a place to put the two of us for the next 10 days that they would be transferring us to Columbus County Jail, so the warden was willing to do that and put us in solitary confinement, and said your meals would be served to you while you're there, but that's better than being pushed into a bad situation. All of the convict's new that we were being transferred out of here.

Allen also told the warden. We got some papers in our cell that we need for our trial for James's case. And if it would be all right to get those important papers, for his case. And when could you move us? The warden said, "We can move you right after supper finisher meal and go back to your cellblock, and I'll send my most trusted guard to get both of you will just tell everyone you both got solitary confinement for breaking ranks in the chow line."

James got his nose all bandaged up once again, and we were escorted to chow and after chow to our cell by a guard to pick up our things. And I got all our papers, and we said our goodbyes to our good friends in cell 172. I told Patrick, I would send Bob to see him on visitor's day when I could arrange it. Next month and would drop him a letter now and then, we got our belongings and the guard put our books on a cart and the other guard wielded as we walked down the long walk to solitary confinement, while the other inmates, made smearing remarks as they passed their cells. It was a long way away on the west side of the compound and it was a very large cell big enough for both of us and not too bad it living conditions clean, with two cots and a wash basin and toilet bowl for the next 12 days our meals would be delivered.

Alan marked the calendar, now the 28th of April. Just 12 more days to go and time for you to get your eighth-grade test on the 5th of May, and you will have more time to study. We got all our books and every thing we need right here for the next 12 days, my young friend, Allen keeps saying that but he's not that much older than I, but it was because of my low education. And my childlike actions. When I came here, almost 3 years ago and now I was only acting more like a man. Allen told me that the few times. Allen said, "It's called growing up, and some take longer, that's all" Even better educated people than you were when you came here, and it's just a frame of mind.

And after we get you cleared of all charges will get you the best education and medical testing. That money can buy, that is a promise I made to you of things long time back. Okay, partner and I was feeling sad and said OK, and the first few days seemed rather nice to be alone and we just kept as busy as we could, during the daylight hours. We had full light. Not from the outside, and at night, just the dim light. At 9 p.m. but if you were in here by yourself. You would be a lonesome thing.

Allen said, "We will just have to keep busy and I know that I am more than ready to defend you in a court and present a winning case in front of the judge. And he practiced in front of me letting me be the judge, and that seemed to be our entertainment so that time went relatively fast." May 1 was now here, and we had no way of knowing what it was like outside and at times, Allen would ask the guard, what kind of the day was my meals came three times a day and reading material and every other day and Allen kipped time on our calendar whenever the lights went dim, but that dim light stayed on all the time during the night was almost enough light in the cell to do some book work.

Just marked the day off on our calendar, and it was no May 3, 1982. On the 5th of May Allen would give me my eighth-grade test. At least that was our plan, and it wasn't much that could change that in here, the guard came once a day and our meals came three times a day the same meal that the other prisoners would get in the mess hall, and James was allowed to go to the infirmary to change bandages on his nose and he would have to go to the infirmary on the day we was to leave here was that plan, and Tony said he got the subpoena and Allen gave a last-minute instructions, and that he would see James on the ninth and re-bandages his nose, and will leave the next day on the 10th and I'll see you in court. So back to our cell we go for seven more days.

CHAPTER 10

Transpierced to
Columbus County Jail

May 5th 1982, today, Allen gave me the eighth-grade test; I passed that test by 80% that was very good compared to what I was three years ago. But then I did a lot of studying to get this far and I now know what the meaning of sex is and rape, and I know the words well. I didn't know the words three years ago, and it hurts me to remember that terrible day, when I was riding my bicycle.

I was riding my bicycle from the Hanson farm, when I went over a hole in the road and skinned my right leg on my bike pedal. And then I found the body of that 12-year-old girl. Yes, the memory will haunt me probably for ever. She was lying facedown no the ground, and I rolled her head over to see if she was breathing - she wasn't. And I said to Allen I. would do the same thing again given the same circumstances. But I was sent to prison for life for being a Good Samaritan, but then everybody should be a Good Samaritan and help other people in their hour of need. That's what the Lord says, and I learned that all from the minister at church here in the prison system.

For the first time in my life, I know about God, and I took a few lessons with that minister, and he taught me a lot in those few classes, and I will go on in life with what I have learned from him. And especially from what I was taught by Allen. And I like that fate of the Protestant church. So I guess I will stick with that.

Allen said, "You need a celebration tonight and I saved of two pieces of cake and two cartons of milk from our meals delivered for tonight after lights out. And he added, only three more days, 80 hours in fact. At least in here, we didn't have to march to eat supper or hear those loud bars crashing as they open the cells. The only thing it was a bit lonely, but if you were a loan. I would imagine almost unbearable way to live.

Next morning, early breakfast at 7:30 a.m. and they brought are trays, and we didn't have to get up by 6:30 a.m. we could take our time getting up, but Allen told me to keep up with my studies on this book I was now working on ninth-grade. He said to be ready for when I am out of here, so immediately after breakfast. I got at my studies, and Allen was working on his bar exam book till lunchtime.

And then all afternoon until supper time and another day is passed and scratched off of our calendar. And then just two more days, and we hope that nothing will go wrong, and another day that Allen said, "At least, we get fed good meals in here, but I haven't been in any other prisons, to make that comparison." That night, Allen said, "Just one more day as he scratched off the calendar. And we give a player together, and that day passed quickly and on the 10th day of May.

That was after breakfast, about an hour after we heard noises coming down the hallway to the cellblock, and then we figured they were coming to get us. And it was a warden two guards who take us to the ambulance service entrance. At first to the warden's office for a final signing of the papers.

And in the ambulance service entrance was a big black van. A driver and two guards, that we were locked in back just for 10 mile hide to Columbus County Jail. As the van pulled within too a closed building, we knew it was the county jail and they hurried us into the sheriff's office. The sheriff seemed like a nice enough person, the sheriff name was Jake Peters about 42 years old. He welcomed us to his county jail and said, "Just in time for lunch boys, and he gave us a list of things that he expected us to do." They opened up a big iron door, but inside was a big room and tables and chairs. You have chairs with a long table in one big TV in the corner, even it through soft chairs and a couch. But this all looked good to us, and there were about 20 inmates, if that's what you call them here. We weren't sure, and I don't think that's what they call people in this place.

They all seemed friendly enough men. Some were just in for short times, one guy was serving a year for drunk driving, and mandatory sentence charge with three offenses in 5 years time, and some were in for assault and battery or family abuse nonsupport those kinds of things. But no hardened criminals in this place, and they were a little afraid of us, once they found out where we came from. That we came from state prison. Allen quickly explained why we were sent here in the excepted is explanation. Dinner was served at the table, and we all sat together as a big group family-style dinner, one man served the food portion was a good meal with good atmosphere, and I learned a new word. I never heard that word used before, and that word will stick in my mind, because I learned words every day from now on what that word was never used before. And later I asked what that word meant.

Individual cells were left open with a nice bunk with pillows and sheets, but were never locked unless you got rowdy. Or got in fights, things of that nature, while Allen said he would get no trouble from us who were allowed phone calls after lunch. And Bob was waiting in the visitor's room and no guards watching over you. Your first private visitor that we had and there was a table and chairs and a private room.

Bob said, "Things will improve in a time, but this is a lot better than were you were okay," Allen said, "Yeah, its fine." Bob said, "I can come any time in afternoons or mornings by a special call. If it's important. I got one piece of news. One woman that was in contact with that guy that make up the blood from Tad Cole, and this woman was a drug pusher. I found out, and she could be the very woman that was there the night of Sandy's death, and I got a blood sample for more off her bar glass. I just took the glass from the bar and send it to the laboratory technician." He said, "He could get a blood type off of that glass. I also give them the original blood sample that I got from Tad Cole.

That makes three blood types in one room that the police said was from that cat, and the women could be the drug pusher. Her name is Laura Thompson." Allen gave Bob, a list of names look on the back page for names of witnesses and other names of interest in James's case. In my cases as well to list, and when will we see our Attorney Jake Warfield. Bob replied, probably tomorrow, because he has the drive 80 miles. So he can't come very often. So I'll set up meetings for you and work out a date, if not tomorrow.

Bob said, "Sure good to have you guys close by," I said yeah me too and Allen said, "Yes it's great to be your already made and we can get my case going faster. After three days, if her blood matches." Bob said, "That's right. I am betting that it does match." And Allen said, "Do you know where she lives," Bob said, "Yes I have a guy following her from time to time, but it's a most dangerous job with these drug pushers, so we got enough on her to prove that she is a conspirator with Tad Cole and other associates of the drug lords and their operations.

We have an enough evidence to blow the whistle on this drug ring in our hometown, and I got a room here not to far away from county jail, and I'll be here most of the time. And here's my telephone number to call, the phone is outside my room in the hall, if I don't hear the call, someone will. And that DNA lab is close by, and I don't have to drive very far, at that laboratory they do other things like livestock cattle sheep and hogs and other testing and manufacturing of artificial insemination material.

May 10, 1982. It was a very long day for Allen and I, maybe we'll rest well tonight, tomorrow we'll see Bob so if I don't get a call from him, then Jake Warfield won't be here tomorrow, you should just be patient. Allen gave him some of our papers, and he would bring us papers, and pencils and even a typewriter. Allen could get our cases all typed up. Or, anything, we needed, like office material and stuff like that the sheriff said it was okay. Just remember that other prisoners and they are not so honest and trustworthy. So be careful about that. The sheriff had told us. Seemed like good advice from places where we were and we come from a dangerous place. And this place was wonderful compared to where we were.

So Bob left and it would soon be supper time. Tonight, we had baked mashed potatoes and gravy baked beans, bread coffee, tea or milk. You could have both if you wanted to kinds of desserts, with Jell-O, which we were used to, yet it was a very good supper, but it was the very first time that James ever saw a TV set, Allen remarked it was amazing to watch him watching the TV. Even like the commercials and he told me, I heard about such sayings, but we had no money to buy anything besides an expensive TV set.

I know I never saw one and its lights out at 10 p.m. and no late show. And we were very tired in a way from our long day of events. And we was able to stay up one hour longer for the first time in three years and this was so much better than the place we come from our first night in county jail, and it felt great. Allen even said so. Our first morning breakfast came at 7:30 a.m. just 30 minutes different in time, but we didn't have to get up at 6:30 a.m. no call from Jake or Bob. So I played some cards with some of the guys on Allen was busy on the typewriter typing up our cases. So the day went by very quickly, and it was now the second day was passed. And tomorrow would be May 12.

Finally Bob called, and said, "Attorney Jake Warfield would be coming at 1:30 p.m. this afternoon." So after lunch, we got all our papers together and were waiting in the waiting room in the visitor's room and he was half hour late. But then it's expected because he lives 80 miles away. He was a short haired, brown eyes, 180 pound shabby man. And I wasn't very impressed. At first sight, and as he continued to talk, Allen wasn't impressed either. So Allen went over the paperwork from the James case. He just seemed a bit defendatory to the sheriff's department, and the District Attorney's department, and everything about the case.

Allen finally said, "Whose side are you on, Mr. Jake Warfield," he snapped back, stood up and said, "Did I have that coming to handle this case." Allen replied. You did not make a very good impression, and it looked you wanted out, and at this time it's too late for me to find in other Attorney to handle this case, I cannot take the case to court, until I pass the bar exam and we are stocked with you, but believe me, Mr. Warfield. You got me to watch over you in court. And I'll be watching every move you make, and you better shown me a lot more than you've just showed at this moment. I got a case for James that any Attorney just out of law school could get it overturned in nothing flat. And now you know, what is expected of you right from the start. And I am the main Attorney and you just follow my leads and will get by okay.

Now Mr. Warfield seemed a bit better, to Allen, and they were talking over things that I didn't understand at all. I brought them some coffee and some donuts that the sheriff's wife brought us and Bob came at 3:30 p.m. and replied I see that you guys are getting along real good, but Allen said, "Yah fine." I look surprised, and I offered him a cup of coffee and a donut that it was nice that she brought us the donuts.

She seemed like a nice lady and she even served the coffee, so after coffee and cake, we got back to our work. I didn't have much to do about anything, but I did ask a few questions. When asked about a certain thing, Allen gave Jake Warfield two lists of names that he had to send subpoenas to including the sheriff's department of Macon County. And the District Attorney's office of Manchester, Georgia and the lab technicians, and it was a long list.

Sheriff Bret Livingston, chief investigator George Bingfang, one of the young police officers name was questionable. District Attorney William W. Warsaw, lab technician Ray Walsh, witness Tony Morrow, Jesse Wright, and Bob Bailey. The farmer's son Edward Martin's owner Frank Martin's Terry Martin's was the one that James talked to on April 15, 1979, one more important witness Alan J. Jeffers. The new lab technician, and there was two of them involved, which you will get the names of which were let go and the new lab technician that will match the blood taken also from the scene samples, and samples of James blood.

We need a picture projector and a screen, and if I have forgotten anyone I'll let you know, and Bob, you can maybe get him a room so he can be closed by this should not take more than 10 days at most. Meantime we got work to do, and you took this case remember Jake, and he replied. Okay, I'll get at it, but Allen implied one more thing. Mr. Jake Warfield. You don't have to worry about my case, because you are not good enough for my case, OK Jake. And he replied you're the boss, as he walked out the door.

By time, they were gone. It was almost suppertime and ending May 12, 1982, May 13th Jake was supposed to be back at 2 p.m. and he was late again. And we had to wait 45 minutes, and Allen was very short with him when he did arrive, and reminded him. We can't be late for court. Of course he had an excuse, while Allen said, "I won't tolerate too much of this being late anymore, and get that room here in town for at least 10 days and be early use the name of the game, from now on Mr. Warfield."

Jake muttered an okay, and what have you got for the day, Allen said, "I want you to go to the sheriff's compound building in Manchester, Georgia and see if you can find James's bicycle that he was riding on April 15, 1979, they never produced that bicycle at the trial. Or you may be able to look in the woods, where the body was found on the scene. But I doubt that it's anywhere, and I believe they have destroyed it." Mr. Warfield's question, then why do you want me to look for Allen said, "I just want to show the court that we made an effort to find it that's all evidence in a case has to be capped in the Department of records for every case that is the law."

And also that one technician from that labbitory was expelled from his job. We think Bob has found him, and the name of that young police officer that made the statement. A slip of the tongue on tape recording, but Allen didn't get his name. And then there is another suspect in James's case. A young man named Billy Walker.

Allen had told me before we left the prison that he found my father, William D. Lundgren, and he was in Manchester, Georgia he was left out of state penitentiary in March 1979, and he was in Manchester, Georgia on April 15, 1979. Bob found witnesses. That said they seen him. We also want those witnesses subpoenaed. I believe Bob has the names, and most importantly, he was sentenced to prison charged with rape of 16-year-old girl. When he said she was willing; and the court ordered him to serve. Not more than six years for statutory rape. He said, "It was not statutory rate, but we made a court order to get his lab test sample to see if it matches the semen found on the victim Candy W. Ploutz.

I was now shocked; If it was possible that my father was responsible for this crime. As I muttered to Allen, and he replied yes it's very possible. And Allen told Jake Warfield, to get the court orders as soon as possible for both of those suspects, and it shows that the police did a shabby job on investigating. When they had reasonable cause, knowing a convict that did reside in that community and was in the area at the time, and they didn't even question him.

Bob said he found where William was shacked up here in town in Columbus, Right now. And the sheriff had another suspect that they didn't even follow up on when the DA ordered to desist. (A, Desisted Case of Rape and Murder) there is no other possible explanation, and we are going to prove it James.

While morning came on the 13th of May. It was a Friday, and to some people Friday the 13th means bad luck. They call it. But then I am not a believer in superstitious things. Allen told me that he didn't believe in the supernatural things of life. And of course I didn't know what the word meant in the first place, and Allen tried to explain it to me. But he said, I'll explain it later, when we got more time okay partner.

Allen added there will always be time to explain everything in court.

While were in trial, so you'll just have to trust me, I'll explain later, if the blood tests, tell us the correct story there won't be much that Crooked DA might even try to get the judge to dismiss your case without a trial so he can avoid the scandalous publicity to tarnish his reputation and also that sheriff's department.

But it is my desire that we have a trial to put these crooked people in their place, and prove that they're not capable of doing their jobs beyond a shadow of doubt, which is their responsibility; and their responsibility, to the public that not only to seek the truth, but to live it as well; in their daily functions of their position. It's inexcusable, and they should be punished for their crimes against you and possibly others.

And that is going to be one of my desires to find out who else they may have sent to prison wrongfully, while they were in office. And my brief I typed up should stand as a legal document. Allen was just telling me before Bob and Jake showed up on time today, but we just had two hours of work. Bob said, "I got that list from the laboratory, this morning, and bingo! We got two matches of blood samples of those blood samples found in the room where Sandy was killed. And he added Allen your case can be quickly dissolved with those blood samples. We filed a warrant this morning at court by the judge that will handle this case of James for the 25th of May in the morning, so it was a good day for Friday the 13th.

And after they were gone, we played cards with some of the cellmates that are what we call them. Allen said, "There doing the legal work. Right now, and Bob is working on a bond to get us out of here shouldn't cost all that much 10% of whatever the judge orders, and a bail bond could be set up for both of us and the cost will be low because we sure wont try to run away when we have such an excellent chance to prove our case, and maybe this can be sent out by next Monday the 16th and won't that be great for the two of us James." To be free from the cell bars that binds us. And Bob has a rooming house for us both to stay and meals would be served right their family style and at the moment, supper was being served. For us and another good meal. There were only 12 of us today, but others come and go for smaller crimes and some here for their crimes and put in solitary confinement detention and chapter 10.

CHAPTER 11

Getting Out of
Jail on Bond

So we had a nice weekend and the first thing Monday morning. Bob came with a bail bond from the judge for the release of both of us and what a happy pair of guys we were. I hugged Bob with tears in my eyes, and he held me with tears in his eyes, and even Bob joined in the hugging with tears in his eyes also. We seemed like three emotional men at the moment, as the three of us held onto each other tightly, and the jailer let us out, was able to pack up are few belongings. We didn't have that much to pack that we packed what little we did have and our first taste of freedom. After three years time that I spent in prison, and five years for Allen.

Bob took us all to a nice restaurant for lunch. Words cannot describe what we both were feeling at this moment. And we ordered a beef steak dinner with all the trimmings. Bob said, "He could afford it and he would be working for Allen, before long ill be doing work that I like doing. And it will be like being my own boss. And maybe even have my own private investigating system someday, it's a thought anyway, for me and to get you guys, some close, and I'll arrange some kind of a loan and will go shopping after lunch."

We took about two hours for lunch and two hours for shopping, everything from underwear to shoes and a few extras like shaving equipment. Even some cologne and the things that we couldn't have in jail were under arm deodorant. And every convict had to smell the order of the other convict. So things like that were important and all that were on the outside. Bob told me that tomorrow, my mother is coming in will be escorted here to see you, I was crying again, I quickly composed myself. And I replied I don't know how I can ever repay you for wonderful things you have done for me, both of you Allen and Bob. Thank you I can't find the right words to express my feelings at this moment. Allen said, "Just finished your education, and they got good schools right here and maybe you should consider renting a small house for you and your mother. I got her a room at the same place, we will be, and she can stay there till trial is over, or tell you can rent a place and eventually get a good job.

It will take time for me to sue the city of Manchester on your behalf, but I can still get you that special school grant and enough money to get by, while you are in school. This is a special school, not just a high school. And those classes are setup according to different times of the day so, you can hold down a part-time job. But that is your choice, but what an exciting day it has been May 16, 1982 a day that will go down in our infamy for all of us. And that also was a word I didn't understand that Allen tried to explain the meaning of that word. Allen said, "Some day, James you will know the meaning of lots of words all the words at your memory can store. And I am setting up my own law firm, right here in Columbus, Georgia. As soon as I passed my bar examination, and that shouldn't take very long."

So after a nice supper at that same restaurant, Bob took all of us to a movie theater for James's first time at a movie. And it was John Wayne in El Dorado. I never saw that one either, I guess it was his newest movie at the time, and after the movie we stopped in a moderate tavern. The tavern was on the corner of the rooming house and in a nice district and Bob bought James his very first beer it was another exciting moment for the three of us. Allen said, "It was five years since he had a cold beer." But we only had three smaller glasses each and back to the rooming house, ending May 16. The best day of my life, but 2nd best was yet to come.

May 17, 1982 each day seemed to bring me more grand and glorious things. It was 5 a.m. as I laid there in this soft bed, and I was just dreaming about my mother. When I was just a young lad 10 years old and she was bent over me taking care of me. When it suddenly dawned on me. She will be here sometime today. It was at least an hour before the sound of Allen and Bob calling me to go to breakfast table downstairs. The landlady Millie

Really put her self out this morning, with a grand breakfast of pancakes and maple syrup eggs and sausage and coffee milk.

She had on a full-time cook to help her, after all she had a big house full of rooms, and we had some good meals also. But it was a great atmosphere and must've been a dozen people at the breakfast table. As I told the landlady, what a grand magnificent breakfast. It really was for all of us and she said, "You sound like a great educated man,

And I can tell you are going to college here at the University; in her Swedish accent voice." And I replied that I would be entering a college Very soon, as possible. But the others came into the dining room, as I told her that my mother was coming today to stay with us for a while, and we are going to rent the house here in town, while I go to the University. Well that's great, she said, "I'll get a special room set up for her on the second-story. And she asked what time." I replied probably 11 a.m. and I ask Allen. If she was coming to this addressed, and he replied yes and he handed me a $50 bill to buy my mother a new dress. And maybe some shoes and what ever goes with it. It's warm enough; she doesn't need a big coat.

I'll just buy her a light coat for now, and she's never been any restaurant and maybe we could take her out to lunch. At that diner, if she gets here in time for lunch on me Bob said, and I ask, where he got all the bail money. And he said, "On a bail bond. You only have to pay a small percentage in case you don't show up. So there wasn't much case in that because he knew we wasn't going to run anywhere with a great chance we had in proving our cases, so just a small fee. And that's all. Allen had to meet Jake at 9 a.m. at the courthouse.

And Bob had other things to do so I was left alone. And I went to the University and asked some questions. They said I could get a school grant easy enough with no income at all and there is a place close by that higher students. Part-time according to your classes, and when would you want to start. And I said, "I would let them know in a few days.

So back at Millie's rooming house mother arrived at 11 a.m. and when her escort vehicle pulled up. I was nervous as a cat I was in the lobby looking out the window waiting. And when she stepped out of the car, she hardly recognized me. I was in my brand-new suit, and she said, is that really you son, I replied, Its me Ma, she replied you look years younger son, as I said, we got big plans for you today, and I handed her some boxes that I bought at the store, wrapped in pretty paper. We were in the lobby now, and you should have saw her face light up when she opened at box raped in pretty paper, with that beautiful dress or three-year separation was awfully hard on her.

But Bob had taken her some money each month to help her with living expenses that I didn't know anything about that. As I said, "What a great human being he really is mother. And just like I was three years ago, she didn't know the meaning of that word, and I explained it to her," and I said, "Mother there's a home course for you and wanted to help you get your education. Like I did in prison. Only in a new house here in town that Allen is helping me to rent or buy very soon. And he is a great man Ma and I know you'll just love him. He hasn't any relatives close by so he can be just like an older son to you, that he is only two years older than I am.

So Allen, Bob, and Jake just walked in the door? I introduced them very formerly to my mother and she was impressed, but didn't know the meaning of the word yet if she didn't know much of anything yet. But Allen was ecstatic about something. When he said, "In two days, I am a free man; the Governor just gave me a full pardon. No trial at all when I produced the blood samples, and he said within 48 hours for paperwork. And I am free as a bird, and he also arranged a bar examination for him self and said if I passed the test. I would be granted a special privilege to handle your case as a legal Attorney for the case of James L. Lundgren. My first case in court all $.50, like we planned; Right."

I answered with a weak voice ok didn't no one else to say at the moment things are happening so fast, it's hard to believe it and mother went to try on her new dress. And when she came back. I couldn't believe my eyes, she looked beautiful, and I said they're something missing. And right after dinner, I am taking you to the boutique for a hairdo and a manicure the works. My mother was now crying, and I had a tear in my eyes also and Allen quickly fixed that. When he put his big arms around both of us. And like he was our father, he gave us both his strength. And we felt much protected. I ask Allen, not to mention my father to mother just now. And he agreed to that for the time being.

Off to dinner we went. The four of us like a family we were, even old sour puss Jake started to get into the family spirit, and he said. Lunches on me, and that was a big gesture and a big surprise so we settled for a group meals served on a big table 2 kinds of meat and all the trimmings. Everything was cooked very well, and Allen said, "And he and Jake had some things to do."

I said I had some things to do also. And they didn't ask me what. And I wanted to surprise them. Later when mother had her new hairdo, and she looked lovely maybe grand is the word, as I saw how lovely she looked, even younger at least 10 years difference, and most people that knew her, would not recognize her at all. And we got back to the boarding house, and Millie said in her Brooklyn and Swedish language, she looks more like your sister, and I'll have that cook makes something special for supper.

You have to have a good meal celebration. I even have a bottle of wine from my sister in Sweden sent me last year for Christmas. And this is a very special day, but she did not know that we came from prison and that we were convicts. And I didn't like lying to her. But Allen said, "It's only a lie, if they asked the questions. Okay." You're right, began, I said, you seem to be always right, Allen said, "I'll bet that District Attorney is squirming in his boots. Right now the Governor said he got calls from the sheriffs Department as well as a District Attorney asking for a full pardon for you, James and wanted to get this case closed out of court. But I want this case to go to court and show how corrupt some of these departments really are. When there's an election, coming up, ending May 18, 1982.

CHAPTER 12

Bar Examination
Before Trial

May 19, 1982, Allen is getting ready to pass the bar examination, to become my legal lawyer. And we still got time to recheck our case; Allen's case has been decided and over. And he will be able to take the bar examination in two days. On May 20 and is very sure he is going to pass that examination, and that he will be able to handle my case as my Attorney, and he is very sure. We have a case that's going to get public attention. Not only that a probable lawsuit, against the county, and the state as well. Allen said, "He was suing the state, for not giving me a proper education, as a child. And that they have failed their duty that every child will get an education, paid for by the state of Georgia."

Not only that allows a chance to put these crooked politicians, like Mr. District Attorney William W. Warsaw; and that crooked sheriff department out of business. Allen calls this the name of the game. He called me last night if you don't fight City Hall for their wrongdoings. Then you become part of that corruption, and thus you become corrupted is bad as the system itself. Just think of the many men that were falsely sent to prison that were sent there that did not do the crime.

True or it may be true that they were guilty of other crimes, but that is beside the point. Alan swore he would not be part of such a corrupted system, and he wanted to do everything he could to stop such things from happening, and he's sure that nothing ever will. And nobody will ever get control of him or his law office. And James you are my first client will get the benefit of everything I have learned as my first case before a judge in Columbus County, Georgia, and this will stand in my lives mood for the future. And I will always defend people that are falsely accused, no matter how much money is offered to subside from the case.

That District Attorney Ordered a Desisted case of Rape and Murder. When there was other possible suspects, and they asked no questions of those suspects. And if your father, Bill D Lundgrenn did this terrible crime that he will deserve full punishment. But that remains to be proved. If his blood matches that found on the victim, Candy L. Ploutz. It becomes the big question? All this Allen told me just last night.

And today I am taking my mother to look at old house on the north side of town that we can possibly rent to own and Allen said we could do that. And of course, we need is legal advice before making such a purchase. But we can look at it, it's on the way edge of town to the north, and there's a wooded area just beyond the small single-story house in bad condition, house with a for sale sign out front. But Allen thought it was a good price and a good possibility to make this our home.

I told mother that I can always do the repairs, and the painting myself. So we took a taxi cab and went out there. I had called the realtor are asking to meet us there at 11 a.m., after we looked at now as I told mother that I could do the work and repair the place and paint the house. After all, I have some experience in also said that might make painting business my life's work. After all, Patrick Franklin taught me everything he knows in prison, and he said he would be willing to take me on as a full partner. As soon as he gets out of that prison. Maybe in a year or less, and may be sooner if Allen gets on his case.

The realtor said, "If you want to move in now, for one hundred dollars down payment will mark down the price to just $6,500. And just $75 a month and they would set up the contract. Of course, I told them I would have to check with my Attorney. It was the single-story house, two-bedroom big living room, reasonable size kitchen, bathroom the hallway closet space and a double car garage, double lot and five acres of woodland in the back and mother I think it's a good deal, but we'll have Allen, check out the paperwork tomorrow.

We can always sell your place in Manchester for whatever we can get for it. Your furniture can be moved for the time being, we can always buy some new appliances. And we will have in a furniture to get by for now. My mother said. James you have really grown up. And I'm very proud of you, what a wonderful man, you turned out to be and not like your worthless father a piece of you know what, he beat me up and drank all our money up before you were five or six years old.

So that was my cue to tell mother that Allen believes he was the one that raped and murdered Sandy L. Ploutz. On April 15 1979, that he was paroled; from prison. March 7, 1979, and was here in town, on April 15, and Allen had ordered a blood sample by the court. And that just is going on as we speak. And of course my mother was very shocked by all of this and said it fits his being that worthlessness. And I believe it is possible and that was her exact words not mine.

As the taxicab dropped us off, at our rooming house in time for a late dinner, of leftovers. The landlady said Allen went back and left me a message and it said, "We got the court order for two blood samples. One of the Bill D. Lundgrenn and the other was Jesse Paullenow; both were in town of Manchester, on April 15, 1979, and both of them paroled March 7, 1979. Almost the same date and both were sent to prison on rape charges. So that was the end of the message. See you tonight for supper, and then I am taken you and your mother out to sea a movie what's ever on. I'm not sure. And in today's I can take the bar examination, end message.

I said to my mother, "Three years ago I couldn't have read that message and Allen has taught me so much. And I promise you mother were going to get you a good education, and while this trial goes on don't be afraid, because there's lots of people that don't have a good education, and taking courses now is very simple. Even people older than you mother, that never finished their schooling. But you have to start at a third-grade level, like I did, but you can do it mother and I kissed her and she went upstairs."

And when she was at the top of this stairs I said where your brand new dress tonight ok. We got a surprise for you. Okay I had the habit of calling her ma, that I said from now on I'll call her mother she deserved the best that I could give her as she went to her room. I did the same and went to mine, and as I lay on my bed. I must've fallen asleep, but my last thoughts were each day was bringing us closer to my case, being finished, and Allen has given me his promise that it will be. And he is convinced me it is going to happen and that I should always look on the positive side. And I couldn't wait to tell him about the house.

When Allen woke me up it was 5:15 p.m., and said supper is ready partner. And wonderful supper it was. And later we took mother to her first movie in her life, and it was Schindler's list. Well, we changed our mind and went to a Western by Randolph Scott, Ride Lonesome. We just happen to like westerns. And mother never would've understood Schindler's list. And I don't think I would've either. When Allen explained it somewhat to some extent, to left why we decided to go to the Western movie. Instead and it would be something simple for mother's first movie. When Allen and I went to the bathroom. I told him that I told mother about the tests. That was going to be made for father, and she told me some things. I never knew before. I always felt that he didn't like me very much. And she said he was a no good, son of a, you know what. And this was the first time she ever spoke bad of my father.

Allen said, "Well just don't let it get you down; you've come a long way in three years. And you're not the same guy. You were when I met you and." I said, well. Thank you Alan," Allen said, "But you needed a friend, and my thanks will be when those people that put you there are punished for their crime. But if you look at this whole matter in a different light. There is a lot of if's here it's if this wouldn't have happened or that wouldn't have happened. And if they didn't send you to prison. Then you wouldn't have met me, and maybe it was just God's will and destiny to raise you above what you were and what you still can be in the future. Hell; maybe you'll grow up to be president some day."

I said, "Well, I got your point. And thank you again," after the movie were stopped in a restaurant for coffee and pie, before going back to our rooming house. And we talked more about that old house, just on the edge of town that mother and I looked at this morning." And Allen said, "You and I can take a look at it in the morning, but will have to put it on hold, at least for the end of the month.

And I got an 11 o'clock appointment. And I'll tell the realtors to hold that house for a few weeks. It won't sell that fast anyway being run down like you said. But I think it's a good enough deal for you to repair. And you're just a guy that can do that." I told Allen about what Patrick said in prison about being a partner with me in the painting business. And I think it's a good idea right, and Allen said, "Ya reminds me, I'll get a letter off to him tomorrow morning, and I think I can get him out in three months or less. I'll be working a new angle for his case that he served enough time already. And a new Attorney can get some attention. And especially being an ex-convict like me, and they know that I mean hard business to them.

And we got those men coming for trial, and I think I can get a message through that infirmary guy Tony Morrow. He will help us I know. Well we finished our coffee and mother was very silent all the while, but I thought she just wanted to give us time to talk. But Allen noticed it first, and cheered her up. Like only he can he is so perceptive is the right word. Well she is just tired, and we better get her home to bed now. We were only a few blocks, but Allen still called a taxicab anyway. After we put mother to bed. We went to Allen's room to go over some things that he wanted me to know, and said he already filed a suit against the state of Georgia.

The suit will be for a non-education. Against the State, that failed to give you the education that it was supposed to give you, and they cannot win this case, no matter what they say or do they lost, and it's just a matter of how much they have to pay. This State school law was many years before we were born, and the grade school law was long before that. And you should have had help your mother when she was abandoned by your father. When you were five or six years old. And although you now have the 8th grade education. The point is they didn't give you that chance to be educated, and therefore the lack of education was what got you into trouble by not knowing that you could have had an Attorney present. While they questioned you. So I filed the lack of child education Law against them that he was not taught your rights as a citizen of the United States of America.

And then they could not have made the case against you that sent you to prison. And then next we sue the county of Macon County, Georgia and that's the bigger case. For more money. I'll start my law practice on my 30%, and the 70% will go to you and you can continue your education. And even go to collage, if you have a mind to go. But that's your decision.

May 20 today, and tomorrow Allan takes his bar examination, but today he asked over all the depositions of what the witnesses are going to say. And he told me that was important to the case to know what each witnesses is going to say. There isn't much for me to do today so I'll just spend time with my mother, and get her started on some third-grade books that I had picked up at the school for her, and she can start in a class. Whenever they set up classes, for elderly people, or people who didn't finish school. And when our trial is finally over.

And to get a set up in a new house, and one problem, I have to pass the driver's test first and learn how to drive a car and Allen said he would teach me. When he has a time, and it would be economical, for us to buy a cheap car for now. And I said, "Mother let's go shopping and to see what's available, and it's such a nice day. So let's walk, and spend the whole afternoon looking. When at the used-car dealer. I ask if I could just try to drive this car, and he said, take it for a drive, will I couldn't do that, because I need a driver license first. The car was a cheap, four-door Chevy 1979 blue color for $700, and any red Chevy pickup. It was a S10, for $750, until the sale ended, that we couldn't buy right now, we were just looking today.

At 4:30 p.m. and Allen just came 10 minutes later, with a big smile on his face, that meant good news. Allen said, "Those blood tests matched your father; and the semen test matched what was found on the victim. So I asked the judge to put him under arrest and the police went to pick him up and locked him up. And when the news got to Manchester, District Attorney's office. He ordered a dismissal of all charges against you and clears your name.

But I told him we were still suing his office and him personally, and also suing The Sheriff's Department, and also him personally. And the county and the state on two charges, and as of now James. You are a free man.

To do what ever you want to do in the first thing I did was hugged Allen; and cried. And my mother did also, while Allen just held us both in is big arms, and held us just like father, would do, and he said, "I also got you a loan set up at the bank, would a checkbook for the sum of $20,000 advance. So you can restore your life and we'll buy you that house tomorrow."

And I told Allen. We looked at some cars today, the Chevrolet car was $700 and a pickup truck was $750. But just how soon can I get a drivers license, Allen remarked, as soon as you can pass the test. So it doesn't take much time, but if you fail the test. It takes 30 days to get another test. So you better be sure your study, that manual carefully. Okay. We'll pick you up some manuals at motor vehicle department, and you'll be driving in no time at all. You'll be able to drive your mother to church to buy groceries. So we had reason to celebrate, and we did right there at the rooming house, Millie made a special supper at 6 p.m. instead of 5:30 p.m. Allen went to the store to get a bottle of wine at the neighborhood store. And we celebrated like a family.

It was 10:30 p.m. before we put mother to bed, and just 12 hours before Allen would take his bar examination. And I ask him if I had to testify at father's trial. Allen said, "Only when we get your cases and my guess is they'll make some kind of offer before any trial. Of course, I'll refuse there offer until I get the right figure and that crooked sheriff and crooked DA are run out of town. That is my goal and he could no longer hold any public service position. That is what I'll hold out for any community needs a good honest, running system not run by crooked sheriffs and crooked DA's. And I promise you, you and your mother will have enough money to live on the rest of your life.

I said to Allen, "I think for the time being, I'll buy that pickup truck. I think, he said it was a 1979, and then I'll be able to haul mothers stuff, and I'll be able to haul my painting equipment, ladders and things like that for my jobs. And I'll start an ad in a paper. As soon as I get a telephone number set up in that house, we're going to buy, and after tomorrow you'll be able to start your law practice." Allen said, "Tomorrow after I passed my bar exam, I will look for an office in the main part of town rent something for the time being and being downtown with a sign out front is better for business. And that is better to attract business."

People all sorts of problems that come to a lawyer for good advice or to make out their wills. Or just a legal contract to buy a house, but I'll hire an assistant to handle some of that smaller things. And then save my time to work at my cases, and I'm going to start with Patrick's case first. I'll have him out in less than two months. But your cases could take a lot of time, so we can't expect any quick settlements. But it all depends and how much they offer. They know they're wrong. There's no doubt about that, but they'll start out what a small figure, which I will refuse.

Tomorrow we'll get you that truck and I'll call that real estate about the house, it was after 11 p.m. before we went to bed. But sleep didn't come to me. I had so much I had to think about, and it must have been 1 a.m. before I got to sleep.

Allen was up early, and we had breakfast altogether, Millie and her cook. Always made something special, but the cooks wouldn't speak a word of English; she was from Germany, and Millie of course was Swedish. Allen said to me that he's got two hours time and will go to that car dealer and get you that truck and will get you that drivers manual to study. And you can practice driving near Millie's and I'll call that real estate company. Right now and will buy that house. I'll make her a deal for cash money and offer her $5,500. And she may take that offer. I understand it's been for sale a long time, and then you can start to paint it and repair it as soon as you get your license or one of Millie's older guys that stay here is not working, and he may drive you wherever you want to go.

So Allen asked Dan Berger, what he was doing for the next week. And if he could start driving James and his mother around, and he said he was glad to do that. So Allen made the call and we had the house, and went to get the truck. And we took Dan Berger right along with us. And I said to mother, you can come along to the house today and we'll get started, and was just fix up two bedrooms, and a kitchen first. But mother said, "She wanted to go every day I can help do the cleaning and stuff like that. Okay and I said okay mother and gave her a big hug and kiss.

After lunch will have Dan Berger drive us to the house, and on the way we stopped at the paint store and buy some equipment, and all the supplies we need to start the job. And I called the phone company to get a telephone number and put the ad in the paper for painting jobs, and I paid for all the materials by check. The first check I ever wrote out in my life and it felt wonderful as it turned out I wrote four checks that day. The first was for the truck.

Dan Berger and mother turned out to be really handy to help with the work. They were very helpful and I asked him if he wanted a part-time job and he was agreeable and quite handy and everything. So we had quite a bit done that after noon. We got the two bedrooms painted the phone company came and put the phone in. At least I didn't have to pay them any check in on the way back to our roaming house. We stopped at a furniture store, and I bought a couple of bedroom sets to be delivered the next day, and a kitchen stove and refrigerator tables and chairs.

That was the fourth check that I wrote out that day, the property had its own cesspool. And well system, but would need a lot of water pumped out to Clearwater in the bathroom was salvageable and workable.

At the rooming house that night. I studied my driver's manual, and it won't take long, and I'll be driving around by myself. Allen got his license to be a lawyer and found an office space. Just four blocks away from that movie theater and just across the street from that diner where we had coffee and pie just the other night.

Allen said, "One to remember James, when you take that drivers test. If you fail, you can't take it for another 30 days so be sure you'll know your signals for turning and also your signs most important and step in at my office anytime, that is a fine there." Okay I gave Allen my telephone number, and I wrote down his number and tomorrow will start a new day. And as soon as I get my driver's license we'll go get mothers things from Manchester. She hasn't got much furniture. That's worth moving so we can probably get it all in one trip.

Allen said, "I'll be starting Patrick's case today, so he should be out in less than two months, at least by July." I said, "I should have my painting business started by then, but I need a name for my service and how about this. James and Patrick's painting servers." Well that sound like a good name Alan remarked.

CHAPTER 13

The State Pays $80,000 for not Educating James

Allen said, "You know what James, we still might have a trial before a judge, on your case, we have to produce records and examinations of your problem. And I know that is a very embarrassing situation for you, touchy subject to discuss what I can get some of that discretion in the judge's chambers. Because of the personal nature involved, but don't expect anything for the next 30 days."

And so just keep that the repair work on your house for you in your wonderful mother and I feel I have gained a stepmother in the process. And I said, "Yes it would be great to have you for a brother, and when I get the inside done, let's have a housewarming party." Allen replied that will be great. So tomorrow will bring another day to work on the House. I expect a few more weeks on the inside of the house, and then can do the outside in my spare time, and yesterday I saw my first wild animal in a field near the woods. It was a doe and a pair of fawns, and I wished I had my camera handy to take their picture and I quickly called Mother to take a look.

Well that was a couple weeks ago, and I called Alan to set up that housewarming party, and he still stayed at Millie's boardinghouse and he should be sure to bring Millie along and Dan Berger would be here, and that's all I know so far, and I got a few small jobs lined up in one big job coming up. But he was not sure about the estimate. But he was willing to give me a 30% differs one or the other. It's a great big old style house, once an expensive place, just North on Pine Drive, just 20 blocks from our place.

Things were going really well for me, and only just starting to feel very confident about myself. And then I would have a good future ahead of me. Allen took me to a specialist on sexual problems, and the doctor's name was Jed Parker and after an examination. He felt surely he could help me with long-term medical care and Growth hormone shots of testosteral, and also injections into the penis itself that will produce somewhat bigger size, but not much can be done about the crushed testicles. But I will never be able to father your child. But he said I would be able to have sexual function as a man with long-term care.

And of course I didn't till mother all about this, because she would not understand it in the first place. But Allen was with me when the doctor gave him his prognosis, and the rest of the times I just told them what one on because of Dr. gave me an immediate circumcision and said it would be very sore for a long time. But that Dr. Jed Parker is hopeful that it will function normally once the soreness goes away, but he said it could take a year or better to have somewhat normal sexual activity, and to produce the desire to want sexual activity. I never knew any of these words, until Alan taught me some of these words in prison. And I'm still going on with my classes. Tonight's a week Tuesday and Thursday nights for four hours, and I passed the great test. And I can start studying now for first-year high school and it will take a long time to graduate. But I am determined.

I told Allen on our party night. When we were alone for a little while and I told him there's a guy just said with a promise that would keep you posted on everything that the doctor would say. Allen said, "The state made a decision on your schooling cost, and I accepted there offer of $80,000, and they included your high school classes."

Even if you went four times a week at four hours per time, that 16 hours per week. And that was a fair offer I figured, and he gave me the check, and you don't owe me nothing on this one, but the others will be 30% like I said OK." And I replied okay that was a big surprise to me. And I can pay up my loan and buy all my painting equipment that I need for my painting business.

Allen said, "In 30 more days, Patrick Franklin would be out of jail, and he needs a place to live and work in order for that parole. But he will have to check in to the local police for parole." I said, "Well, he can stay right here with us on the lots of rooms in this big old house, and it will be great to have him here, I'm sure mother would enjoy the company and wouldn't mind doing the cooking."

So we went back to our party. For more refreshments, only beer in one bottle of wine, Millie liked wine, but mother had just to ship. After all, she never drank anything before, and I showed mother my check for $80,000. I said this is from the state for my education, so everyone shared, and we celebrated till 1 p.m. and everybody stayed over the night. It was a Saturday and on Sunday morning, I wanted to take mother to church that I had joined. But I still had to take church instruction, and mother could join also and would have to take instructions also to become a member of Nazareth Lutheran church of Columbus N. Division St, and it was a smaller membership, and it wasn't too far away. We could even walk if we wanted to on Sunday, it was now June 6 1982 so after the service. I introduced her to the Reverend and he said she could start instructions at the same time that I was taking instructions to make it easier for us.

So when we got home everyone was gone, so mother made dinner, and while I was looking out the window that doe and her fawns came out in the corner of the field to eat corn from what I had put their, a few weeks ago. It was now a daily routine. Even bought mother a pet, a black Labrador dog, very young to watch over mother while I was gone the next week I got my driver's license. And told mother next week will go to Manchester, and it are things from our old place, and it will be our very first trip. Good for mother, but strange for me to be back in that place. It seemed a lifetime ago to many strange memories all flashing through my mind at the same time. Like in a dream, and I woke up, and it was a dream at 3 a.m. somewhat frightened from what I just was dreaming. Never before I had such mixed up emotions about anything.

Monday June 7, after a good breakfast made by my lovely mother, I went to my job I only got 5 rooms to do on this job, and I was working alone, I was using all latex paint so clean up is quicker. And quick drying time also and washable. I had two rooms done by noon, and went for lunch at the restaurant by Allen's to meet him for lunch at the dinner a crossed from his office. I told Allen this week end mother and I am going to get her things from Manchester and get her stuff. I rented a trailer in case I can't get every thing on the truck.

Or maybe I'll just buy the trailer, he said he wanted $200 for it but I'll see how it runs it's got a spear tire. Allen said, "I got to meet some people in Manchester also on Friday lets go together ok and stay the night ok." I agreed, Allen said, "I got to see the Governor on a matter concerning Patrick case.

And if they are willing we might get Patrick out sooner, than expected." I replied that will be great, and he can work for me and eventfully be my partner; Allen said, "Not tell his parole is final that takes 60 days, then just check in first once a week and then once a month." Ok I replied no problem, so our lunch was over and I went back to work.

I told Allen I would pick him up on Friday at noon we could have lunch at Sam's dinner be for we start out for Manchester, Allen's appointment was at 4-30PM so we'll have plenty of time.

Friday at 11-30 A.M. we left our house we now love dearly and we are both proud of our place, we got to Allen's down town office at just be for noon, we had a nice lunch and started out for Manchester, just less than 2 hour drive, we were there by 3-15PM. We took Allen to his meeting place. And mother and I went to our old place north west of town; I had bad memories instantly all coming at me in fast motion like a whirlpool.

I told mother about what I was thinking about at the moment, but it past by as quickly as it came. I called the real state people to come and list our house for sale, and lets not sleep here tonight ok mother, I got to many bad memories here coming at me, ok mother said. I said, "Lets just box every thing up that we can today your canned food in the basement we can pack carefully, but there is a lot of stuff to take out side and burn, lets just burn most of the stuff ok mother.

So really wasn't that much to pack up we boxed up every thing we could by time we were to meet Allen at 5-30PM and it won't take to long in the morning to load up, so the real state person came and listed our house. We got to the court house at 5-45 PM to pick up Allen and he said he rented a motel for the night for us, and a good place to eat just a crossed the street for supper. At supper Allen told us the good news that Patrick could get out of jail by next Friday, we can pick him up at the entrance of the prison at 10:30 a.m.

I said, "Let's give him a homecoming party at my place. Okay," sound like a darn good idea. Allen remarked a coming-out party is just what he needs. But he has to check in with the local sheriff's office first, and the Governor; was so surprised when I showed him the report that 95% of the prisoners. In that state penitentiary had no high school education at all, and 55% of them didn't even have grade school diplomas. And also I told the Governor that this was unexceptionable to society that it was the state's responsibility to educate every single person, no matter what is race creed or color, and I suggested too have schools right in the present system. And he said it sounded like a good idea, and that Governors said, "This is going to be the first state in the United States; to do this new practice to educate all prisoners with at least a grade school level with those that are willing to participate and I said, "That sounds great Governor."

And other states could follow this practice as well, but the point would be how too get Congress to help with this project, and that Governor gave me a good idea to make a run for office myself. Anyway, it's a thought, and it came to me after I left the Governor's office. And I would call the Democratic senator, Delbert Swanson sometime soon. And when I will call him about this project, to see what he thinks and what could be done, and later when I called him. He said he would see what he could do to organize a bill of that effect. In this may be good news for all other states to follow our lead.

Allen said to me how your homecoming was. I replied we had a bonfire and burnt most of the stuff we had. So I don't need a trailer after all, mother saved a few things, and we got them packed up inboxes and Allen replied. What's for supper? I said, how about a big 2 inch beef steak, Allen replied, sounds good to me mother said she wasn't that Hungary sol make mine smaller. I haven't had a beef steak for many years, and Allen replied. We'll fix that right now, as he held mother in his arms for a moment and mother kissed him on the cheek. As we all sat down for supper and we made this good meal last a long time. It was 8 PM before we got through and went to the motel. We had adjoining rooms, and one bathroom and a good hot bath is just what we needed, and good night sleep. While mother was in the bathroom, I told Allen it won't take long to load up in the morning, just 15 boxes of canned food and stuff that mother collected at last two or three years, blankets close and personal stuff of mothers.

Mother replied, let's make a turkey dinner for Patrick, and that was the second time she called him just Pat and I replied your right mother, and Allen said he would bring the pumpkin pie. And don't forget Millie and Dan. So there will be seven for the coming home party.

So in the morning we loaded up my truck, didn't take long and headed on to our new home with great anticipation for the future. That Allen made possible with his kind and loving heart. Such men are hard to find in this world today. Leaving the past behind us that was so devastating for me, that I felt relieved when I left it, I turned around and took my last look at the house where I was born but not feeling sad that I was leaving. Only with a tear brought to my eyes as I hugged my mother tightly, and said to the future mother and a new life, and a little prayer silently. And I can't thank him enough for what he is done for me. As I turned onto the highway heading west towards our new home. I used the old prayer I was taught by a teacher by the Reverend in prison system. Forgive us Lord, because sometimes they know not what they do. So look to the heavens above for your new requiem of life. Just a short prayer in silence.

I don't think Allen or mother knew what I was thinking at the moment, as we now pulled into our driveway of our new home. It was 3:30 p.m. I had left Allen off at his office and we could unload what was on the truck by our self. I parked the trailer by the grudge, we didn't need it this time, but it would come in handy in the future. That's for sure, and I thought I'd buy it anyway. He only wanted $200 for it, and I'll use it sooner or later, as I said to mother. "We got four days to plan that party for Patrick. Let's call it a homecoming for Patrick." He was nine years in that state penitentiary so he will need some help adjusting to private life. It's a terrible thing to serve time when you know, you are not guilty of the crime, that you are serving time for.

So how big of a turkey do you want mother, I'll buy one on Thursday, so make out your grocery list okay mother. I had a small job for the rest of the day, and Dan will help you unpack the rest of the stuff. Okay mother. See you later.

So anyway those four-day just flew by, and I bought a 14 pound turkey and all the things that mother wanted from the store and some refreshments. Just beer and pop and one bottle of wine for Millie. And on Friday morning real early Millie wanted to come and help mother bake that Turkey and between the three of them. They were busy most of the day, while Allen and I went to pick up Patrick. The prison time was 10 a.m. when he was 30 minutes late, but that's usual for prison systems, but it was a good site to see him no suitcase. Just one old suit, I told Allen, we should take him shopping first, and he agreed with me and it was a grand reunion sort of wonderful to see him. Free at last, after serving nine years for something he said he didn't do. When he gave us a high greeting and some tears all the way around, with a welcome words and are hard to describe those feelings unless you were there your self.

So we sat side-by-side in my little pickup, and the first stop was at the store to buy a suit of close and some work pants, shirts and shoes the works. White overalls for painting jobs, T-shirts and underwear, one suite you do go to church in. At least he didn't need a haircut, as prisoners are cut very short on regular basis; there are actually two reasons for cutting your hair short. One is for cleanliness, the other is so some other prisoner can't get a hold of your hair and break your neck. They taught us that in the prison that the enemy could break your neck by getting a hold of your hair. We spent about three hours, buying Patrick's close and it was 3:30 p.m. when we got to my place. My mother never met Patrick. But she hugged him like he was no stranger with tears in her eyes for him. And they talk to each other instantly and mother had a strange look in her eye that I never had seen before.

Allen had stopped off at his office and would come later, supper was to be at 6 p.m. was the plan, Patrick and I had time to reminisce old times. When we were in the state penitentiary. We had a can of beer or two. There was no need to help mother in the kitchen with the help she had, the three of them were like professionals. When it comes to cooking a big meal and the rest of us could just set and drink a can of beer. Allen came about 5:30 p.m. we had taken Patrick and checked into the local police station at 11:30 a.m. and he would have to check in the first one a week for the first month. And then once a month for six months, and then he was permanently paroled and on his own.

What a grand party it really was with big Patrick, with tears in his eyes hugging my mother. It was a sight to behold. The memory, one can only share with good friends. And he also said, how he can ever repay Allen for all he is done for him, and for me as well. But then Allen is that kind of a guy, but I said to Patrick. We start working tomorrow on an old house on Hickory Street, and Patrick replied okay boss and I replied. It's just temporarily for six months.

The three of us men were telling Daniel all about prison life, while drinking a can of beer. He looked a little tipsy. He said he wasn't used to drinking anything, and Millie wanted to go home at 11:30 p.m. and Allen thought that he better take Dan home, and Patrick and I and mother stayed up for another hour, mostly cleaning up the house, and Patrick enjoyed helping mother do the dishes and what a grand sight it really was to see him standing next to my mother. And when they were done mother said that she was very tired and went to bed and Patrick and I stayed up for another can of beer.

I said, "Patrick if you don't sleep well on that nice clean bed. Call me and let me know. I got some sleeping pills from Dr. Wald, to help me on some of those nights when I have trouble sleeping. And I gave him two tablets, in case he needed them. But he replied, I think I'll sleep very well tonight. First time in nine years, I had four cans of beer. Or any beer, for that matter, and I'm feeling just a little tipsy. When I say this but I love you and Allen, like a brothers. And I would cut off my right arm for either one of you and I wanted you to know that as he said goodnight. And I replied. It won't be that early, maybe 9 a.m. so don't worry about getting up to early. He replied, you know, we've been getting up early for nine years. So I'll probably wake up at that time anyway. I said yeah, mother is an early riser. Also so you can chat with her, I might sleep an extra hour, as I didn't get much sleep last night, good night old friend.

I put Patrick in the spare room downstairs in my room was upstairs and mother had the master bedroom on the ground level. This house was built with one room up stairs just like a loft. I usually have the alarm set for 6:30 a.m. but mother said she wouldn't call me tell eight for breakfast. She thinks it's the most important meal of the day, and I believe she is right, as I finally drifted off to sleep. My thoughts where of tomorrow's job, and the two of us together working on a job, that he taught me how to do in the first place.

And mother called me at 8 a.m. Patrick was already in his painter pants and white shirt. And as I joined him for breakfast in my white overalls, his were brand new. After I said good morning. We got just a small job to do today, before we start that big house on Hickory Street, and imagine what color she picked. Emerald green that's the color I got to mix up. Today enough to do that job about 20 gallons ought to be enough; I told Allen we would meet him for lunch. Across from his office at Sam's Place, and he said, "Looks like you guys are now on the working force," and Patrick said, "Very hardly. In fact. And it's for a really good change."

Allen paid the bill for lunch and handed Patrick a check for $2000, but said he wished it would be bigger, until he would get his case settled, and this will all they could get through the parole system. But for one year, you are in my custody. The own way I could get you paroled, but if I prove my case and prove that you were not involved. And that's a statement in itself from one of the robbers that did the killing of that station attendant. And you are not the accomplish to the crime, and you got five to 10 years. And you serve nine of those years.

We got you out only one year and two months earlier, but when I prove my case, you will be paid for those nine years by negligence out of the law enforcement of your township where you lived all your life. But that's going to take some time, so be patient and will see you guys every day for lunch. Okay.

So after lunch, I took Patrick to my bank where he could open an account and he put half in a savings account and the rest in a checking account and the first check he wrote out was to me, for his close. And he wanted to pay it. He wanted it that way so I didn't argue with him. But I told him. From now on the labor for every house would be split. 40% for him and 60% for me to pay the insurance bill and other remaining bills that occur from our company and the Social Security payments to the state on both of us in business has to be run in that manner, and the way you do your book work. But it's only temporarily; till we form a partnership and we worked those papers out later in six months from now.

Well it won't be much to forming a business partnership and work will increase as we get new business all the time, and you can stay right at the house with mother and I and I'm sure she doesn't mind. I think she likes you, she said this morning. I like your big gentleman.

Patrick said, "I am 44 years old in two months from now and you mother can't be much older than I am and I liked her instantly." Patrick was a good-looking big guy, when neatly shaved and dressed and I wondered if maybe they sparked a little interest of romance. My mother even looked pretty good now that she was dressed good and took better care of her hair and I sent her to the beauty shop. Just a week ago, and she looked very good with lipstick and some rouge. Like women supposed to look at is hard to think of your mother as sexual or something like that. And I didn't know much in that department anyway.

But the doctor said, "It would take about a year before I got any sexual desires." And I wondered what it would be like, but the doctor is sure that it will come some day, and to be patient that he will famous word of Allen's while we were in prison. Be patient and his long as I stay on that hormone shot every 21 days and later it would be once a month. That would be a year from now, but if you're a male person with a little sexual function and take Viagra. Maybe you will know what it may be like for a man like James, who never had any sexual desire. In his life now almost 23 years old.

We spent about a month on that big old style house, and the day we finished the house. She wrote a check for $24,000. That was the first big house, so far in the business. I said, "Patrick we really should celebrate again, we'll ask mother that question? When we get home mother had supper ready for us more leftover turkey, she had frozen for a while, and she and Patrick were on first name basis. She called him Pat, and he called her Marry I said to myself. Patrick and Mary, that makes for a good pair after supper was over Patrick insisted on helping with the dishes. So I left the two of them to do their finished cleaning work. And I sat down and read the paper tomorrow is Sunday, and I got Patrick interested in joining our church.

And Sunday we all three went together for the second time since Patrick has been with us. We don't use the word prison very often in our daily talk. It's something we both like to forget. And I told him. Nobody needs to know why church about your background. You're just a friend of mine that came to town looking for a job. At church mother sat between us like we were both her sons. But I think she looked at Patrick with different eyes, and maybe a little romance sparked her loving soul. And now I know all about those things and someday I may get those feelings as well. The date was now June 7, 1982, nobody at church asks any questions about where Patrick came from. And I asked them in a group that we could join our classes on the same night in the Minister said that would be OK with him.

Patrick insisted on paying room and board to mother, whatever they worked out something reasonable and next week. Wednesday night, we could all three of us go to this church for class. My mother and Patrick were getting very chummy like a spark of romance might take place at any time. It's hard to think of my mother and Pat as being my stepfather. Well I guess if that happens I'll accept it. Even Alan had a date. The other night, and the doctor said, those feelings could come to me before the year goes by, to just be ready when that really does come to you and you may have a sexual erection. And then maybe a sexual relationship could form, but it will have to come naturally and slowly for you, but there is no way to restore those crushed testicles; and for that the doctor gives me a shot of testosteral every 21 days and then I have to work on my excepting those feelings that are produced by that drug and right now my penis is still so sore from that circumcision. And I have to put a lot of salve on it three times a day.

Patrick and I will form are company, partnership in just 50 more days and we are getting lots of work. And Allen has already drawn up the contract ready for us to sign when the time comes. And until then, there's no reason to change and living arrangements, and each day brings us closer to that partnership agreement.

But Allen keeps telling me it could be six months yet, but it will come. He says, and I believe him full heartedly. And mother and I have our house now fully decorated and furnished and no debts and money in the bank drawing interest. Life is really good to me and to my mother and to Patrick, and I feel he is part of our family; those are big changes for the three ex-convicts. All from cellblock D. cell 172 from state penitentiary.

My routine day is based on work that we have two do work that we have lined up and a few nights a week we go to church study classes studying catechism, I am ahead of most of them, but it doesn't make much difference. Now, June 15, and of another week and services on Sunday, and another day of rest. We don't work unless it's absolutely necessary, on Sunday that someone demands a job being finished or something like that.

Something special for both of us, and we both bid every job, and we hired a new man, to help us on the job, and he was our only employee. His name is Fred Jenkins; a young fellow was just lucking for a job needed it badly. And we put him on temporarily for a long as we have worked for him, but we got a few new houses to do this winter outside and inside as well, wood staining and stuff like that.

Each day that goes by, I see my mother looking at Patrick with the romantic eye, and vice versa. So I expect my mother will set the tone for the relationship to start. And where it might lead to any way I have to trust her that she knows what she's doing. And she is still taking her course in the fourth grade class 8 hours per week, but she finds the time to make us good meals and keep our house running smoothly.

Patrick only has to check in the police station now once a month. And then once every three months and then the final end of his probation is now in the end of June, and we are planting a Fourth of July celebration for our group of eight and Allen said, "He was bringing his girlfriend." So that makes nine our group is getting bigger all the time and mother and I planned it all day cook out, I bought 5 pounds of brats, and I couldn't help thinking of my last Fourth of July. When I got my nose busted for the third time. But the good thing was we met Tony, and he helped us a great deal. While we were in prison. Allen keeps in touch with him and he finished his internment ship in that prison system. This January 10, 1983, and Bob is a full-time investigator set up right here in Columbus. And we invited them for our Fourth of July party.

He said he never did find my bicycle. They must have destroyed it, or someone stole it off of the spot they claim. Allen is very busy each day, but we meet him. Almost every day for lunch at Sam's Place and reminisce old times. And yes we can reminisce about the hard times. We spent in state penitentiary and Allen said, "The best part was. It brought the four of us together, which I believe God intended that somehow our destinies was molded shape together, long before we met."

I invited our young employee to come to our party Fred seemed kind of lonely and didn't know anybody else in town, nor did I ask him about his background, that was his business. And he could tell me what he wants to go, so Fourth of July was a grand party time for all of us.

CHAPTER 14

July 4th Party Was a Success All Us Jail Birds Were Working Full Time

And I said let's do it again next year. Every Fourth of July we'll have our party, and they all agreed to that. And I felt a little bit overwhelmed by my feelings. When Allen's girlfriend, kissed me on the cheek. My head tingled with an elation that soon overwhelmed my entire body. She looked very sexy as Allen put it, and I thought so also. And I suddenly had feelings that I couldn't explain and later I tried to write down exactly how I felt. So I could tell my doctor and he told me what to expect some time, some kind of erection to take place and he also could increase the dosage in my shots of testosteral. If those feelings were occurring. Very often, and he wants to know exactly what's been happening to me at all times. He knows that it is working and wants to know exactly when I get an erection of some kind. And this was a definite erection again know what to do about my emotions. And at the start of an erection, because Allen's, girlfriend kissed me on the cheek.

So I made all my notes later to tell my doctor at my next visit. And I was excited that I got my first erection in my life. Over this girl that Allen brought to the party. I didn't know how to tell Allen, but I did because he wanted to know. He was very interested in my progress. And I told him when we were in a bathroom together, and he said, "Good now you know

102

that it's working. And you well start to have other feelings as well, and it's perfectly normal, but that's where your morality comes into play. Self morality is taught to you by a minister's.

The Christian side of a person's life and the morality code is taught by other institutions like school and your personal morale's, takes over lets you know when it's proper, and when to make proper advances towards the opposite sex. And surely not someone's wife or girlfriend, of a good friend and I assume you'll learn plenty of that in church. And your politics come into play, along with your morality; because your politics are what you are. What you believe in your personal views. No matter what side of politics, takes over your life is something you will have to work on as time goes by, to be on the right side is important to yourself as a man of what you believe in. And as far as I can tell, Allen said, you show signs of being a Republican. Like I am myself."

Allen said, "There is a big difference, and politics Ronald Reagan for one showed us the difference gave us good leadership for eight years and brought the Russian Communist Party to a close when he told the Russian leader Khrushchev. When he said, the famous words? Mr. Khrushchev, (Tear down This Wall); and by the grace of God. They started to tear down that wall; that was built; starting back in 1945 after VE Day and what a glorious day it was for all American people and around the world. And James, you will learn all about this kind of politics.

So July 4 was over, and back to our usual days routine of work, school and church all fill's our days with hopes; for the future and the rest of the month just flew by, with nothing special. And by the end of August, we signed our partnership between Patrick and me. Allen had the papers all drew up ahead of time, and he also said he was close to a settlement with county, but the case against the District Attorney was going slowly. He was setting up a lot of roadblocks to the case, which ties it up for another 30 days.

One day I stopped by a sports shop. I was seeing that nice buck in my field, and I talked to the sport shop people about a bow, and was a 50 pound Pearson bow, with 60 pounds let off. And I told them all about my young eight point buck I was seeing in my field, and I was able to take a few practice shots. So I bought it for $185. In that same day Patrick and I built a tree stand in a corner of my field. And I started to practice every day from that tree stand platform. Patrick would set up cardboard, deer cut out target the season would open September 15.

So on that date, I was sure that I could hit what I aimed at. And just a half hour before dark, this young eight point buck walked up to my stand, and my arrow went through both lungs, and he jumped out, just like he was not hit at all and I got down for my stand again with lots of blood on the spot. And I could see the buck lying just 30 yards back in the woods. I was quite happy as I looked at him laying there. And I called to Patrick to come and help me, I knew nothing about gutting a deer out, and that sort of thing, and Patrick said. He never did either, so any way we got the job done and hung the buck up. In my garage to cool down over the night. I wanted to mount the full head of this beautiful eight point buck. So I called the taxidermy that was close to me and he said he would come over and skin. The whole thing out for me, and mount the head. And I think, he said $200.

End of September, Allen called and said he had a settlement from Macon County, in the sum all of $150,000. So I said will have to celebrate again, Allen said, "Lets do that. And in another month or two will have that crooked District Attorney out of business. They gave him 30 more days in office, and then he's gone and we should get another $150,000 from him and his office a personal damage for his Desisted case of rape and murder, against you and don't be surprised if its sooner than what I just said. He surely wants to avoid a public trial, and all that embarrassment, and that crooked sheriff's department as well, we might get another 50,000 out of him for his part in this fiasco of sending the wrong man to jail because he took part of this Desisted case of rape and murder. And never even picked up the suspects that were just released from prison for the same crimes they sure a dereliction of duty by an elected official. And neither one of them will ever be able to hold office in this state.

So late that afternoon, Allen came to my house with those checks, and by end of December. You should all be over. I showed him the pictures of my nice first eight point buck, and Allen remarked that he never got the urge to ever go hunting. And I said, "I really like hunting, and this will be my sport from now on, and they want me to join their bow shooting club league this winter." And I told Allen. I had another erection just the other day in a restaurant this sexy waitress walked right up to me where I could look at her boobs. And it happened. I couldn't understand all the feelings I had, but I knew I had to control myself.

Allen said, "Well good for you, it's sooner than your doctor said it would be. You just can't let nature take its course. You have to be prepared for any of your actions and you a lot to learn how to seduce a young girl and start a friendship, first and then maybe a sexual relationship can start okay." I replied yes, I know I have a lot to learn about my own sexuality. If that is the right word, and Allen replied, that is the exact right word. It was now end of September 1982. As much as happened since last September, when I got my nose broke for the four-time Allen replied. Yes, I remember it well, and it's all right for us to commemorate those activities, because we were in the right, and they were in the wrong.

Allen thinks in a few months, everything will be settled. I am looking forward to my education and a take my classes very seriously compared to some of the others I have learned a lot in just a short time, and everyday I learn a new word, and I look up the meaning of that word. The word today was ironic, if anything in the world could be more ironic than what just happened to me the last few years. It's even very strange to say the least strange ironic event, and I used the term very explicitly because of the nature involved.

Starting with my father, who gave me life than he ran off and left me to fend for myself with my mother's limited education or means of supporting me. I had to quit school in third grade and get a job. Then that same man that was my father got out of jail rape the little 12-year-old girl and killed her in the process on the same day that I was riding my bicycle back from the farmer in which I applied for a job so I find the body of the little girl laying alongside of the road. And like a Good Samaritan. I make the telephone call to the police and then they turn around and arrest me for the crime sent me to jail for life in which I met a wonderful man like Alan by chance. And he uses every bit of his knowledge and experience to get me out of jail.

And then Allen proves that it was physically impossible for James to have raped and killed that little girl. And later, the DNA tests showed that it was in fact, my father that he raped and killed this little girl. It's a strange irony. So strange that one won't hesitate to believe that someone could be sole uneducated as I was at that time, April 15, 1979, and know my father is in that same prison that Allen got me out of you as yourself the question. Even in 1979, could anyone have been to use the word loosely stupid isn't a word, ignorant or anything you want to call it what you believe that even today in our high-tech world we live in today.

There are still some people, that dumb and ignorant or whatever word you want to choose. Sometimes you just have to look in the right places. I know some people that are living in our high-tech world of today, without change, and they are living like they were back in the 50s. But Allen said, "The best thing that came out of the strong destined ironic story was. The four of us got to be friends. And we'll all go on and live productive lives, regardless of our terrible ordeal." And it's all right to think about these things from time to time. Allen taught me how to think for myself and help me get educated to the point that. Now I want to learn more about myself and others around me.

There's no way I can ever repay him for what he has done for me. But all he wants is my friendship and for me to rise above, what I was. And I am learning more every day of even just common things. I might want to go on to college, but I have enough money to invest and I'll give that more thought. But for right now I'm contented to just be a painter and enjoy my friendship with Patrick.

And the doctor says, those erections will come more often than what I have to do and expect some sexual reaction in a few months, I got acquainted with that waitress, and we struck up a good conversation. A few times, and I ask her for a date to go out to supper, and then a movie. She accepted, as her shift is over by 6 p.m. so I'll take her to a nice restaurant, first and then a movie at 9 p.m. and from there. I don't know. But Allen said. Just don't let it happen to be alone with her yet tell you know, you can function naturally as a man. And it's too early yet for that, I ask Alan, what I could do if she wants to have sex. And I can't get an erection, and Allen said, "Just tell her you're a Christian with a high set of moral values. It should work every time and don't take her anywhere private.

I am also looking forward to November, when deer hunting season will arrive. I bought myself a lever action 3030 Winchester. I'll hunt on my own land. I couldn't talk Patrick into joining me. But mother and Patrick are starting to date, and in her own way and you should just see them together. Just as natural as ever, looks like they were just made for each other. Is the word, and I accepted it. And by spring may be there'll be a wedding. Although my mother is low educated. She knows about morals, values and the proper way to conduct she self as a woman. The only thing I ever saw of them doing is just kissing each other. A few times, Mother night talk only a couple times about father, and she said, we don't ever have to talk about him again. He is out of our life and in the place where he belongs. Those were her last words.

I mentioned this destined ironic event to mother the way Alan described it. And I study all about that at school, and I asked questions of the teacher at least a lot more than the other students do, but the teacher said he likes people that asked questions. I keep all my paperwork together for future reference, and I am slower than other students at learning and need more help. But he did that gladly to me.

Just yesterday, Allen told me about his study about the prison system and the statistics of low educated people are in prison. He gave a set of numbers, that was like 70% of the prison system was only up to eighth grade level and a big margin, although his 70% did not have a grade school diploma and among the black and Hispanic. The numbers were even higher. Even among other races of people Native Americans or Asian, the numbers were even higher. So Allen is going all the way with his plan to change the future prison system and that takes time.

But we meet every day for lunch, and he keeps me posted on what he is up to, and he takes his job very seriously and won't rest until he gets it finished. He is highly motivated and passionate about that job. I think I used the right words to describe just how he goes about his activity. He is an excellent lawyer, and he is just starting his political movements as a Republican alderman in our district. And what always he might even wind up Governor of our state. He told me the old Governor is gone now, along with that crooked district Attorney and Sheriff's department. They are no longer in business, and he expects two more checks in the early future.

As for me I am practicing every day with my new rifle. I got two bucks on my property that I saw just last night. One seems to be 10 points, and the other is just a small four points, and last night was a doe and two fawns. Anyway, it's a few weeks yet till November 15 that is opening day for deer season.

Patrick and I finished the new house exterior, and we started on the second one that has to be done. To do the inside this winter, we don't get a lot of snow in this part of the country. And it doesn't get too cold. But it's still winter, but right now it is still pretty warm weather, and we are able to work outside most everyday for a while yet anyway, but the jobs keep coming for us, and that's good news. And most every day, we meet Alan at Sam's Place, for lunch. But then a few days, when Allen can't make it because he is out of town or just too busy.

He said he had a state senator, on his program to help what education on the list of every prison in United States. At least were starred in our state, and we all look forward to that day for all the men and women that are incarcerated in prison systems. Allen told me that 80% of the women in state penitentiary at lower of an eighth-grade education and over half of them and Lower than a fourth grade test and that only 20% had high school diplomas. That could pass the test for that level. So I believe Allen and on the right track here for this project, and he will take it to the end.

Just like you would take my case, a Desisted case of rape and murder. And they now want a trial, but Allen made his point to the judge in just a short time in Judges Chamber. He showed the judge, a pitcher all of me taken in the dispensary of the prison by Alan and Tony and the pitcher focused on my lower genitals and said your honor. Do you think, the man in this photograph could possibly have raped anyone and the judge took a good look and said no? You made your point. You make your case and no need for a trial if the sheriff's department would have taken James L. Lundgren to a laboratory and made these tests that you made in prison on this defendant. There would have been no case and no conviction by me or any other judge and he awarded you $100,000 from the sheriff's department and $50,000 from the sheriff personally.

And those checks will be forth coming in the few days and your case is over as far as court is concerned. And I will use some of that money to fight my case, to better the education system in prison. That brought forth this ironic tale of events, but your father will get the benefit of these education systems while he's in jail. Strange ironic event and we don't talk much about it at least about my father; it came up in our conversation.

I'm a rich man by any standard, but I think of myself as just a hard-working painter. I will finish my high school education, and will see what develops after that, Allen has asked me to be a spokesman at his convention. And I answered, he didn't know how to do it and Allen replied, you can learn just like you learned everything else. And I believe you can do that. And it is very important to my case, to have living proof. Allen implied, and it's my way to pay him back some for all the things he has done for me.

CHAPTER 15

James's Lucky Day

November 15, Saturday morning was my tremendously lucky day. I went to my deer stand 20 minutes before daylight and 20 minutes after daylight. Here come my Big 10 pointers, he walked right up to me. Just like the other one did when I had my bow, one shot, and he was down. I called Pat, and he came with the four wheeler, and we strap my buck on and drove up to my garage. My mother wanted pictures of all of us together and luckily Allen came at that exact moment from the city with two checks for me one for $100,000 from the sheriff's department. And another one for 75,000 from the sheriff himself. And I held both checks up for the camera, what a glorious day it has been mother fried us all some venison and eggs for breakfast. And we enjoyed the morning together. I wrote Allen out a check for his percentage $61,000 for his share of that money.

He said that Patrick's case would still be pending right in the end he would still get him a nice check in time. I call the same taxidermy to common skin my buck out. And he sent some one over immediately. And we all watched while having a couple cans of beer, Allen laughed and whispered to me and said, "What do you think this guy would say right now, if he knew all three of us were cellmates in cell 172 in state penitentiary."

I said, "Let's not put it to the test. I haven't told anybody anything. It's our secret and were entitled to have that secret, and nobody ever asked me anything so far, so I really didn't have to lie yet, but I will when the time comes, we are surely entitled to protect our self with the secret right. And he replied, right he said, also were just three leading citizens, and it looks like a right now, hunting citizens.

Allen replied. I won the November 5 election, recently and the recount was coming very slow, but now I am elected fifth Ward alderman and the next step is a state representative. So this was a happy day for everyone, not just me and mother had the greatest news of all. When she said Patrick has asked her to marry him. And she wondered what my thoughts were about a wedding day. By December 15, and I said to that's great; I gave my mother a big kiss and hugged Patrick like a brother, I replied, let's have a can of beer to celebrate this great occasion, and the four of us were very happy.

Later on in the bathroom I told Allen, that I had a date with that sexy waitress and I feel ready to have a sexual relationship with her and her name is Susie Kidman. And I'm going to give it a try; I rented as a motel room for the evening. And anyway, this is my lucky day in more ways than one, so that night for my first sexual experience. I wanted it to be very private. And what's better than a motel room downtown.

I started the evening out with a good supper, at the most expensive place in town. There was a band there would little dancing, and a few drinks to loosen us up. And I just learned to dance about two weeks ago in my spare time, which wasn't much these days she had a couple cocktails and I just had a can of beer. I did want to get drunk and spoil it and then at 11:30 p.m. I took her to the motel. I was a bit clumsy, but she was the expert and helps me through some how she knew this was my first time I ever had sex. I know I told her that once, but I didn't think she remembered. But somehow I got the job done. I don't know what, if she was satisfied or not, but she seemed very happy about it and we stayed there the entire night.

And in the morning we had one more go round, and this was about four months sooner than my doctor predicted, and I felt like calling him early in the morning and telling him so I decided he can wait till noon at least on Monday. For that kind of news, but I did call Alan early Sunday morning and went to pick mother up for church. She didn't know I was out all night. She could not hear any movement from her room. So she didn't know what time I got home. Nor could she hear me enter the house at any other times. I gave her a big hug this morning, and the three of us went off to church, and for of first time in my life, I felt like a man, what strange feelings was going through my mind and my body first time in my life I knew what it was like. Can you imagine what it must be like for a person like me to finally have what most man? Have at maturity.

And what most men take for granted, it's almost unbelievable, and unexplainable in words. Because of all the feelings that a young man goes through while growing up, and has to sort out all those feelings from the time he's 13 years old, and if he doesn't have the proper guidance. At that time, it can be devastating to a young boy looking for maturity and some boys are just a little bit slower depending on early maturity, and it's been known that a 13-year-old boy that produced a child. He was in between 13 and 14. I remember the case, when I heard about it. And later they even made a movie about that case. And when the baby was about a year and a half, he was 16 now and got custody of the child and thus he became a father at an early age. A man with responsibilities, and he took those responsibilities seriously, and with the help of his parents. He succeeded in raising his child,

Here I am, at the age 26 and first became a man in the sexual department, but sexual activity is a big part of being a man, and early teachings gives you all your mature kindness or gentleness or being cruel. These are all parts of bring a man that what kind of man are you. Your motivation, every aspect of your life is involved around sexuality. In some form or other. And that's just another reason why they're making studies in prison systems about education and sexuality.

Allen has told me of some of the studies that are going on in the prison systems, and that were made and the numbers are shocking for our society and unacceptable that the under educated men and women that fill our prisons. Because of the low education factor. Our next big percentage number in prison is sexual problems, prostitution and sex offenders, and child molesters. Family abusers, alcohol and drugs, would you believe there is less bank robbers.

Take my own father as a matter-of-fact, he was a sex offender, and finally, he killed, and raped that little girl Candy Plowtz. By not being able to understand his own sexuality, and being a low educated person, adding the two factors. It's an explosive situation, a time bomb ready to go off, if one wants to put it in the worst terms. And in some states. They have the death penalty for such crimes, and also for the crime that I didn't commit. And now my own father would be put to death for that crime. And in some states psychiatrist are just starting to make more mental tests of prisoners as they come into the prison systems and women alike in finding out that these statistics are just unacceptable.

Some could argue the tests for accuracy, in some prison systems for in general. But some of these test stand undisputed that education and sexuality is the two most common and most logical subjects of why this number of people are here in these prison systems.

Allen some day wants my story published. And I told him I would get someone to help me write my story. And he thought he could use my story. In his fight to get justice done, and education a part of ever prison system in United States. If only just the grade school level for a trial, And also sex education would go along with that bill that comes from the Senate. That would offer sex offenders a way to understand themselves and their own sexuality, and to know why they did such hideous crimes against society and against individuals in our society as well.

They're also trying to analyze why, educated people get in to prison systems and mainly it's just greed or bankrupt people turning to crime. Or just have a bad credit card debt hanging over their heads.

It's now December 1982, and I was just reminiscent in some of the old times and thinking about a year ago when I was in prison, and I first learned the meaning of the word Christmas. And what it meant to every person and child in the world. And that I learned this in the prison chapel. I cut a Christmas tree down from my own woods and bought my first box of tree ornaments, and my mother knew very a little about Christmas or church for that matter, and no money he made it limited all such activity for and her only child myself.

My mother and Patrick were planning a wedding for early December. And they will get married in our own church, with just the five of us for the wedding party. I took them to the best restaurant in town. I even bought mother a beautiful white dress, well it was almost white with a touch of blue. And I gave the bride away and my mother was very happy. And I cried, the entire time, I guess I'm just an old softy at heart supper and an expensive diner. And I felt proud that I could give my mother a good wedding dress, and everything that went with it. Not everybody that can give his mother away at her wedding at age 26. And what a grand experience, it was in reality; she was married to a man from cell block D cell 172 of state penitentiary.

I now had a new life, and a new working body functioning like God intended, and a brand new brother-in-law and a good lawyer. And my good business running with plenty work, and money in the bank. Might be a good catch for some nice young gal. There just one thing, I wouldn't be able to give her is a child. Yes it's true we could adopt some children, and I don't have to be truly honest with her that I could not father a child, because if child did spawn out of that relationship, there would always be doubts and suspicions, on my mind; and know marriage, can survive that. We have to be very frank and open about my situation. But right now, I didn't want to share this with anyone. Not even my mother, I started to once but then could not find the words to finish. I started to get tongue-tied and have to give up because I could not find the words to describe my problem.

Patrick knows a little bit of my problem. And I told him to keep it a secret, and to himself. And I hope he will do that. My cases are now all settled, and I even had in a notion the other day to go and visit my father, who is now in state penitentiary. But I wanted to face him man-to-man. I talked it over with my minister at class, and he agreed that I should do that. Just for my own reasons, but I made no different plan. I told Allen about it and he said, "Wait till you're stronger and able to explain everything. And what you want to say to him. He's just going to laugh in your face anyway, I saw him one day, but I hated to tell you, because he appears to be such a terrible man.

I don't know much about money investments, and I saw an investment broker. Just the other day to help me invest some of my money, but I didn't make no deal. It seemed too impossible to understand it. I found someone to help me write my story, and I wanted to write that story from the time I was born. Up until now, I was able to put most of it down. And then he filled in parts that I couldn't explain as I described to him. And I was totally honest with him. His name was Gary Harkins, as I would get one chapter done he would rewrite that chapter from my thoughts. We can only spend a few hours a week. And sometimes a Sunday afternoon.

Mother insisted that I stay home with her and Patrick. Mother thinks I should have to call him Daddy. It's just a joke, although he is my stepfather by law. I find it hard to think of him in any other way than just a good friend. And now my mother's husband. And so much as happened this last year, one could hardly imagine everything that took place in that year's time. Devastating things that lives in my own infamy, and that wonderful destiny that brought Allen to my life. And those things stand out very clear in my mind. One could draw a conclusion that this story has come to an end what better words. Can one use to except the truth? Allen told me that once, that the truth shell set you free, and he was right. It set me free and brought me a new life full of hopes and dreams. As Allen puts it a well-deserved life. I can't describe the words that I was feeling at this moment. I surely will have a productive life as a newfound Christian of fate. My fate is slowly binding me to those factors that only God can perform miracles. Thank you for reading my story. A dream I had March 24, 2010. The end.